THIS BOOK
BELONGS TO
aLEX Williams-jan-
nis.. . . . .

SELBY SCREAMS

BY THE SAME AUTHOR

Selby   Secret
Selby Speaks
The Ghost and the Goggle Box
The Ghost and the Gory Story
The Ghost and the Shutterbug
My Dog's a Scaredy-Cat
Comedies for Kids
Spy Code Handbook
Piggott Place

SELBY
SCREAMS

DUNCAN BALL
ILLUSTRATED BY ALLAN STOMANN

📚 Angus&Robertson
An imprint of HarperCollins*Publishers*

An Angus & Robertson Publication

Angus&Robertson, an imprint
of HarperCollins*Publishers*
25 Ryde Road, Pymble NSW 2073, Australia
31 View Road, Glenfield, Auckland 10, New Zealand

First published in Australia by Angus & Robertson Publishers in 1989
This Bluegum paperback edition published in 1991
Reprinted in 1991 (twice), 1994

National Library of Australia
Cataloguing-in-Publication data:

Ball, Duncan. 1941-   .
   Selby screams.
   ISBN 0 207 16728 1.
   1. Dogs — Juvenile fiction. I. Stomann, Allan.
   II. Title.
   A823'.3

Typeset in 14pt Plantin by Best-set Typesetter Ltd, Hong Kong
Printed in Australia by Griffin Paperbacks, Adelaide

9 8 7 6 5 4
97 96 95 94

This one's for Eliot

CONTENTS

GO!

Just a few words about this book before you GO ahead and start reading it. These stories are for people who like talking-dog stories. I mean, it isn't the stories that talk, it's the dog — me.

They all really happened to me and I told them to the author.

(I could have written them better myself but I get writer's paw when I write a lot.)

As you may already know, my real name's not Selby and the people I live with aren't really the Trifles. If I told you who I really was I'd never get any peace. You know how it is.

Selby

FINISHED IN A FLASH

"What a great camera!" Dr Trifle said as he whipped around and snapped a picture of the bewildered Selby. "It's amazing! All you have to do is point it and press the button and it does everything else. It focuses itself and decides if it needs the flash and it even winds the film!"

"That was a close call," Selby thought, as he looked up from the newspaper he'd been lying on. "He almost caught me secretly reading. I've got to be very careful with Dr Trifle snapping pictures with his new Inig-Matic camera or my secret won't be a secret for much longer."

"Look at all these exciting features!" Dr Trifle said, reading the camera brochure about all the buttons that could be pressed and dials that could be turned. "It's even got *Smile-Sensitivity*!"

"Smile-Sensitivity?" Mrs Trifle asked as

she wondered why men were so interested in pressing buttons and turning dials. "Does that mean you'll hurt its feelings if you smile at it?"

"Nothing of the kind," Dr Trifle said. "It's something special that lets you press a button on the back of the camera and then run around to the front and it takes your picture— but not till you smile. Isn't that great!"

"And what if you don't feel like smiling?" Mrs Trifle, who was watching a movie on TV about an orphan who was lost in the snow, asked.

"Then it'll refuse to take your picture."

"Refuse to take your picture?" Mrs Trifle said. "How dare it? I may be old-fashioned but, the way I see it, cameras should do what you tell them to do."

"That's all well and good for your normal run-of-the-mill camera. But these new cameras have minds of their own. If it's set for Smile-Sensitivity you'd jolly well better smile or it'll just jack up and that's that, no picture."

"Perhaps I'm missing the point," Mrs Trifle said.

"The point is that cameras don't lie."

"Is that so?" Mrs Trifle thought as she tried to remember if she'd ever been lied to by a camera.

"That just means that if someone is feeling

sad or looking terrible or something it'll come out in the photo. But if you click the Smile-Sensitivity button, this one will only take happy photos," Dr Trifle said as he clipped his Super Bug-O-Rama magnifying lens on the front of the camera. "Now I'm going out to the garden to get some pictures of insects."

"But we've got to go shopping now," Mrs Trifle said. "Besides, how will you ever get a bug to smile?"

"That's silly," Dr Trifle laughed, and with this he spun around and took another snapshot of Selby, almost catching him reading again. "You don't turn on the Smile-Sensitivity when you're taking pictures of insects."

"This thing's driving me crazy," Selby thought, picking up the camera when Dr and Mrs Trifle had gone shopping. "I can't do anything for fear of being photographed. Even if I'm lying innocently in front of the TV Dr Trifle might take a picture. When it was developed he might realise that I was actually watching the TV."

Selby pushed some buttons and turned some dials on the camera and then picked up the brochure. It showed a picture of a camera sliced down the middle and lots of arrows pointing to things.

"This camera *does* have everything," Selby

thought, getting more interested by the minute. "It's even got a shark alarm for when you're taking pictures underwater."

The thought of swimming underwater with the Inig-Matic dangling from his neck suddenly brought a smile to Selby's lips and— just as suddenly—there was a blinding flash.

"What was that?" Selby said, dropping the brochure and hoping the flash was lightning striking or a light globe burning out. "Oh, no! I forgot about the *Smile-Sensitivity*. It's taken a picture of me reading the brochure! When the Trifles see the photograph, they'll know I can read! My secret will be out! Help! I've got to do something fast!"

Selby lunged for the camera to destroy the film but just then Dr Trifle burst in the door.

"My goodness!" the doctor exclaimed as he grabbed the camera from in front of the flying dog. "The film is finished. I'll have to send it away to Celia's to be processed straight away."

That night Selby couldn't sleep.

"I'm sitting on a time bomb," he thought. "As soon as Dr Trifle gets his pictures back in the post, he'll see the one of me reading and my days of freedom will be at an end. Oh, sure, at first it'll be all friendly. They'll ask me what it's like to be a dog and I'll tell them how horrible Dry-Mouth Dog Biscuits are and they may even give me some of their own people-food to eat. Then, gradually, there will be things to be done. 'Selby, would you mind doing this and would you mind doing that?' Before I know it, I'll be their servant! I want to be their pet, not their servant. Or worse still, they'll send me off to a laboratory where I'll have to talk to boring scientists all day. Oh woe, woe, woe. The only sensible thing is to snitch the photo and the negative before Dr Trifle sees them. But how?"

For the next few days when Postie Paterson put the mail in the Trifle's letterbox, Selby was watching from the garage through Dr

5

Trifle's binoculars.

"That's it!" Selby said at last when he saw the unmistakable yellow envelope from Celia's No-Scratch Photo Service. "Now if I can only get to the envelope . . ."

Selby crept out to the letterbox and nudged the lid up with his nose as he often did when he brought in the mail. But just as he was about to grab the envelope, a hand shot in front of his face and beat him to it.

"Never mind, Selby," said Dr Trifle, who'd also been anxiously waiting for Postie's delivery, "I'll get it. Yoooohooo!" he called over to Mrs Trifle. "Come and have a look at the photos!"

The sweat dripped from Selby's forehead as Dr and Mrs Trifle looked through the stack of photographs.

"Isn't that a good one of you?" Mrs Trifle said to Dr Trifle.

"What do you mean?" Dr Trifle said. "It makes me look terrible."

"Well they say the camera doesn't lie, dear," Mrs Trifle chuckled as her husband flipped through the pack.

"My goodness! What's this?" Dr Trifle suddenly exclaimed as he looked at the last picture.

"I do believe it's Selby!" Mrs Trifle said,

6

looking over at Selby who was lying innocently on the ground.

"I can't stand it," Selby thought as he cleared his throat. "I'll have to tell them. They've caught me. I'll have to confess. Gulp."

"But how could he have taken it?" Mrs Trifle asked.

"Well I don't know," Dr Trifle said, frowning at Selby. "Maybe he just bumped against it and *flash*! it went off."

For a minute, Dr and Mrs Trifle's heads went back and forth from the photo to Selby like two people watching a tennis match.

"It's really quite extraordinary," Mrs Trifle said. "I can't imagine how it happened."

"I must have left the Super Bug-O-Rama magnifying lens on the camera," Dr Trifle said. "It just looks like a close-up of fur with a tiny piece of his collar showing. What a laugh."

"Thank goodness," Selby thought as he breathed a great sigh of relief. "Cameras may not lie but luckily for me they don't always tell the whole truth either."

NUMBER FUMBLER

"Remember when the council chose the town of Twin Castles in Tallstoria to be our sister town?" Mrs Trifle, who was the mayor of Bogusville, asked Dr Trifle.

"Yes," Dr Trifle said. "As I recall, the mayor of Twin Castles was planning to come here for a visit sometime."

"Not just sometime," Mrs Trifle said. "Count Karnht and his wife, the countess, will be staying here for the night tonight. They're due at five o'clock."

"How exciting! I do hope he speaks English. I don't speak a word of Tallstorian."

"Count Karnht speaks perfect English but he has trouble with his numbers. He has a way of saying two when he means one and three when he means four and so on."

"You mean, Count Karnht can't count?"

"Yes. He grew up very rich and always had other people to count for him so he never learned. But Countess Karnht can count and she's written to tell us to ignore anything that her husband says that has numbers in it."

"My goodness," Dr Trifle said, as a huge black car with flags on it pulled into the driveway. "I think it's them!"

"The count that can't count can't tell time either," thought Selby as he noticed the royal couple were two hours early.

"Let's not be formal," Count Karnht said, kissing Dr and Mrs Trifle on both cheeks. "We're not here as the royal single—"

"He means the royal *couple*," the countess whispered to the Trifles.

"—but as the mayor of Triple Castles."

"He means, *Twin* Castles," the countess said. "And I *do* apologise if we're early or late. My husband said we were due at fifteen o'clock and I took a blind guess that he meant three."

"It's six dozen of one or half of another," the count said, suddenly seeing Selby and screaming: "Help! Get that three-legged creature out of here! I was attacked by two packs of them when I was a boy of thirty."

"But Selby wouldn't hurt a fly," Mrs Trifle said.

"I don't care how many flies he wouldn't hurt," Count Karnht said, jumping up on the table. "I can't cope with dogs. My wife used to keep canines but we had to get rid of them. They frighten me out of my wit!"

"You mean, your *half* wit," Selby thought as he slinked out the door which Dr Trifle held open for him. "Now *I've* got to sleep outside just because Count Karnht who can't count can't cope with canines."

Selby went down to Bogusville Creek, curled up in a bush and slept for a couple of hours—which would have been okay if Count Karnht hadn't come along on his evening walk and stood throwing stones in the water.

"I can't seem to get away from him," Selby said to himself.

"Another dog!" Count Karnht cried, seeing Selby and jumping into a deep part of the creek.

"What a ninny," Selby thought as he got up slowly and stretched. "I guess I'd better get out of here before this turns into an international incident."

"Heeeeelp!" yelled the count.

"Now wait a minute," Selby thought as he turned to go. "The count's gone under and he hasn't come up! In a minute he could be the drowned Count Karnht!"

Selby watched as the count bobbed to the surface and thrashed around with his arms.

"Learning to count wasn't the only thing the count didn't learn to do when he was young," Selby thought. "It seems he didn't learn much about swimming either."

Selby thought for a minute about diving into the creek and grabbing the count by the collar.

"It'll never work," he thought. "He's too frightened. He'd just pull us both under. I could hold out a branch for him to grab," Selby thought, spying a long branch lying nearby, "but no matter what I do, he'll know I'm not just an ordinary dog! My secret will be out! But I can't let him drown ..."

Selby grabbed the branch and held it out but the floundering count was too frightened to grab it.

"Don't panic, your moronic majesty!" Selby said suddenly. "Just grab the branch!"

"Good gracious!" sputtered the count. "You talked!"

"Never mind about that," Selby said, leaning further out.

Selby pulled the count to shore just as the whole of the Bogusville police force—Constable Long and Sergeant Short—came running.

"What's wrong?" Constable Long asked. "What's the fuss?"

"It's all right now, officers," the count said, coughing out some water and wiping his eyes. "A nice dog frightened me into the water

SELBY SCREAMS

but then he rescued me so it was okay."

"You were rescued by a dog?" Constable Long said. "What sort of dog?"

"A dog sort of a dog," the count said, looking around for Selby who'd run back into the bushes. "You know, the kind with five legs."

"A five-legged dog?" Sergeant Short asked.

"Yes, of course," the count said, combing his hair back, "and three ears and two heads. You know perfectly well what I mean and don't pretend you don't!"

Constable Long pulled out a pad of paper and a pencil.

"Let's see," he said, making some notes. "You were rescued by a dog with five legs, three ears and two heads. Just an ordinary dog, was it?"

"Good heaven, no!" the count said sharply. "There was nothing ordinary about him. He talked to me in perfect English."

"He *talked*?" Sergeant Short said.

"He certainly did. Now, if you don't mind, I am His Highnesses Count Karnht, the mayor of Quadruple Castle in Tallstoria," Count Karnht said, pulling out a soggie mayor's ribbon and putting it around his neck. "I'm staying with your mayor, Mrs Trifle. Now take me to her house on the triple."

The two policemen stared at each other in disbelief.

"Oh, so you're Count Karnht who can't count," Constable Long said.

"That, certainly, is I," the count said, standing up very straight.

"Very well then, Count, we'll take you back to the mayor's house. I know it's in Bunya-Bunya Crescent but I've forgotten the number," Constable Long said, winking at Sergeant Short. "You wouldn't remember what it was, would you?"

"Why yes, I think I do. It was either a thousand hundred or nought two six. Either way I know it had an eight in it," Count Karnht said as he climbed into the police car. "It's a pity that dog left so quickly. I wanted to say, 'Thanks.'"

"I'm sure he'd have wanted to say, 'You're welcome,'" Constable Long said, holding back a giggle.

"I'm sure of it," the count said. "Now let's get going. My pant is wringing wet and so are my shirts."

"Fortunately the count and countess will be leaving tomorrow morning," Selby said, as the police car drove away. "So, in the meantime, I think I'll just stay here and catch thirty winks. *Thirty winks?* Oh, no! Now he's got me doing it!"

A HAIL OF SNAILS

"Jetty has asked us if she could have a get-together here, in our own backyard," Mrs Trifle said. "She's invited the Friends of Furry and Fishy Animals. What she wants to do is get some money for her next animal-collecting expedition to Africa."

"But do you think she's up to braving the hardships of the African bush?" Dr Trifle said, looking up from a gadget he was making which looked curiously like a lettuce.

"I don't know," Mrs Trifle said. "And I'm afraid the FFFA have their doubts and won't be giving her any more money. She'll just have to be prepared to take no for an answer and pay her own way."

"I've never known Jetty to take no for an answer yet," Dr Trifle said, adjusting one of the lettuce leaves with a tiny screwdriver. "She's a very persuasive woman. She could charm a snail out of its shell if she wanted to. And if she can't charm them, she'll use some other method of persuasion, you wait and see."

"Charm, schmarm," Selby thought as he lay on the carpet thinking of the dreadful woman. "She's about as charming as a vampire bat. I wonder what Dr Trifle means when he says she'll use another method of persuasion?"

"Speaking of snails," Mrs Trifle said, "we'll have to get all the snails out of the garden by Thursday. Remember, Jetty goes quite bonkers when she sees them," Mrs Trifle added, referring to the time when thousands of falling snails nearly pummelled her to death in a rainforest at the very moment she was being attacked by head hunters.

"Funny you should mention snails," Dr Trifle said, holding up his new device. "This is my Snail Slinger."

"What does a Snail Slinger do?"

"Just what its name says, it slings snails. Come outside and watch."

Selby and Mrs Trifle watched as Dr Trifle put his invention down in the middle of a small lettuce patch and then pulled its leaves back till they clicked. In a minute a snail had made its way onto a leaf and with a terrifying noise that sounded something like *whump-whizzang!*, only louder, the snail shot up into the air and out of sight.

"You see," said Dr Trifle proudly as another luckless snail and then another was launched into the air, "it's friendlier than poisoning them and it's quicker than taking them across town in the car and then letting them go. Besides, I can never get them to leave the car when I open the car door."

"It's all very well to launch them into the air, dear," Mrs Trifle said, holding her hands over her head, "but aren't they likely to come whizzing right back down?"

"The Slinger is designed to always send them into someone else's backyard. If they make their way back, *kabam!*—or rather, *whump-whizzang!*—they're gone again. I'll leave the Slinger here and the garden will be snail-free by the time the FFFA arrives on Thursday. Goodness me," Dr Trifle added, "I haven't had a success like this in years. I'd better make a few more test models just to be sure everything's okay."

On the day of the garden party, Selby climbed into a bush in the backyard to listen to Jetty's talk.

"This is the moment I've been waiting for," he thought, "the moment when—for the first time in her life—Aunt Jetty *doesn't* get what she wants. Oh boy! I can't wait!"

"Ladies and gentlemen of the Friends of

Furry and Fishy Animals," Aunt Jetty began. "Let's be frank. I want money for an expedition to collect animals but you think I'm not able to brave the hardships of the African bush. That's a big load of rubbish!"

There was a murmur from the audience followed by a lot of whispering.

"I want to tell you," Jetty boomed, slamming her walking-stick on the table so hard that the table broke in two, "that I'm as fit as I was when I was twenty—and when I was twenty I could wrestle a five metre croc and come away smiling."

Suddenly Selby heard a distant sound that was something like *whump-whizzang*! followed by a long whistling noise.

"My goodness," he thought. "That sounds curiously like the sound of an airborne snail."

The snail bounced on the ground and Mrs Trifle jumped out of her chair and hid it before Aunt Jetty could see it. Just then there was another *whump-whizzang!* followed by a whole bunch of *whumps!* and dozens of *whizzangs!* and Mrs Trifle raced around the yard frantically gathering up falling snails and hiding them in her handbag.

"Excuse me, dear," she whispered to Dr Trifle, "but what did you do with the other

Snail Slingers you made? The ones you were going to give to the neighbours to test out."

"I gave them to all the neighbours to test out," Dr Trifle said, ducking another flying snail. "Ooooops! I can see now that that may have been a bit of a mistake."

All at once the air was filled with *whump-whizzangs* and the sound of whizzing snails raining down on the Friends of Furry and Fishy Animals like gooey hailstones.

"What *is* going on here?" Aunt Jetty said, looking up and seeing that the sky was black with snails. "What are those—?"

Suddenly something in Aunt Jetty snapped.

"Head hunters!" she screamed, grabbing a man who tried to run past her and knocking him to the ground with her walking-stick. "I'm surrounded by head hunters!"

"She's flipped her wig!" Selby thought as Aunt Jetty waded into the crowd, picking people up at random and throwing them around like so many rag dolls. "She's done her lolly! And, furthermore, she's ruined her chances of getting money out of this mob! This is great!"

In a few minutes the snail-rain had slowed to a trickle and the ladies and gentlemen of the FFFA who hadn't followed the Trifles into the house lay groaning on the ground.

"What happened?" Jetty asked as she staggered around in a circle, slowly coming to her senses. "Have I beaten back the attack?"

"Don't hit me!" cried the president of the Friends of Furry and Fishy Animals through two black eyes. "You proved your point! Here!" he said, quickly scribbling out a cheque. "Take the money and go off to Africa. Don't wait till morning, *go now!*"

"I'm not sure that you'd call that *charming* them," Selby thought as he scurried out from under the bush and into the garage. "Dr Trifle was certainly right when he said she had other methods of persuasion."

SELBY'S SELLING SPREE

"Selby's been chosen to do that TV commercial!" Mrs Trifle said, reading the letter that had just arrived.

"I wonder why they chose Selby out of all those pedigree dogs they saw?" Dr Trifle asked.

"Maybe because I was the smartest, handsomest dog of them all," Selby thought as he grabbed a Dry-Mouth Dog Biscuit from his bowl and remembered how impressed they were when he stood on his hind legs, barked, jumped through a hoop and did all the other silly things they asked him to do.

"They say they chose him because he looks so average," Mrs Trifle answered. "Sort of a dog-next-door kind of mongrel."

"'Dog-next-door?' Charming," Selby said as he gagged on the dog biscuit. "I guess I'll have to show them a thing or two. When I finish with that ad it's going to be so great that they'll sell squillions of dollars of whatever it is they're advertising. Hmmmmmm, I wonder what the ad is for."

The next day Mrs Trifle drove to the studio in the city with Selby. Inside the huge room was a set that looked just like a kitchen. There were bright lights, TV cameras and people dashing everywhere.

"Thank goodness you're here, we're ready to go," the director said to Mrs Trifle, patting Selby on the head as if he was bouncing a basketball. "And aren't you a perfect little doggie. You're just the sort of homely mutt we need. I only hope he likes Dry-Mouth Dog Biscuits because that's what the ad is for."

"Oh, no!" Selby thought. "Of all the products in the world, why does it have to be Dry-Mouth Dog Biscuits! I want to do an ad for super-expensive soap. I could lie in one of those enormous bathtubs with a telephone next to it. I could brush my teeth till they sparkle. Why can't I drive a car over rocky mountain roads? Why can't I fly on Happytime Airlines and have a friendly stewardess fluff up my pillow and give me one of those cute little airline meals? Why oh *why* does it have to be an ad for Dry-Mouth Dog Biscuits?!"

"He loves them," Mrs Trifle said. "He eats them all the time at home."

"And will he come when he's called?" the director asked.

"Will I come when I'm called?" Selby thought. "The man thinks I'm a mental midget."

"I think so," Mrs Trifle answered. "If you're polite about it, that is."

"Well it doesn't matter. If he can't handle it, we've got another dog in the wings we can use," the director said. "Sort of an understudy—or should I say an *underdog*."

"Very funny," Selby thought. "I can handle it. Now stop batting your gums and let's get the show on the road."

"The only person in the ad is the actor, Tim Trembly," the director said. "I'm sure you know him from his films. As a matter of fact," he said, lowering his voice, "we're a bit worried about Tim. He hasn't acted for many years and he's a bit nervous. He'd like to get back into acting and he knows if this ad comes out well he'll be offered lots of acting work. It's very important to him."

"I remember his films from when I was a girl," Mrs Trifle said. "He had such a beautiful voice. All my friends were secretly in love with him."

"Tim!" the director called out, motioning to the silver-haired actor who stood nervously holding a cup of tea. "Come and meet Mrs Trifle, Tim!"

"Tim Trembly! What a wonderful actor!" Selby thought as he watched the old actor walk across the studio floor, tripping on cables as he went. "He hasn't acted since that film that everyone hated, *A Dry Month at Dog Bay*. I thought it was okay."

"Here's what we're going to do," the director said to Tim. "First you open the door and call out, *Here boy!* Then the dog comes racing into the kitchen and starts eating the biscuits. You kneel down and pat him and say, *My dog knows good dog biscuits when he sees them. If he could talk he'd say, Dry-Mouth Dog Biscuits are for me.* Got it?"

"I think so," Tim Trembly said. "It's just that I'm a little n-n-nervous. So please be patient with me."

"You'll be right," the director said. "Now let's get rolling."

Mrs Trifle led Selby out the back door to the kitchen as the camera operators moved the cameras. There was silence for a moment and then . . .

"Here, boy!" Tim called out.

"Wow! How exciting!" Selby thought, as he pranced in the open door. "Now to show them some real acting."

Selby walked towards the bowl of dog biscuits, stopping for a fraction of a second, looking around casually and then turning his head slightly to let the camera see his better side. Then, with a flick of his eyes towards the camera he reached down and started delicately chewing the corner of a dog biscuit.

"My goodness!" he heard the director whisper. "It almost looks like he's acting! He's perfect!"

"If he could talk," Tim went on, "he'd say . . ."

The camera moved in on Selby's face and everyone waited anxiously for Tim Trembly to finish his line.

"Cut!" the director yelled finally. "What's wrong? Just say, *Dry-Mouth Dog Biscuits are for me.*"

"I remembered the line," Tim said. "But I just couldn't say it. It sort of stuck in my throat, if you know what I mean. I don't know what's wrong with me."

Again and again Selby pranced into the kitchen and Tim Trembly began speaking his lines in his beautiful flowing voice. And again and again Tim stopped dead just before his final line.

"Poor Tim," Selby thought as he glanced up and saw the actor's trembling face. "If only they knew I could talk, I could say his last line myself."

"Cut!" the director yelled. *"Dry-Mouth Dog Biscuits are for me.* It's simple. Just say it, Tim. We haven't much time left."

"I'm sorry," Tim Trembly said, close to tears. "I'll try it again."

This time Selby gave it everything he could. He even grabbed a biscuit in his lips and then threw it in the air, catching it squarely in his mouth. But again the old actor got to the last line and stopped.

"I know what's wrong!" Selby thought. "He'll *never* be able to say that line. *Dry-Mouth Dog Biscuits are for me* sounds too much like the name of his disastrous movie, *A Dry Month at Dog Bay.* The film was such a terrible experience for him that now he's got a mental block and he can't say anything that even *sounds* like the title."

Suddenly, as Selby chewed his way through another biscuit, a devilish thought crossed his mind. Then, just when Tim came to his line and struggled to say the words, just when the director was about to yell, *Cut!*, there came a clear flowing Tim Trembly-like voice that said: *"Dry-Mouth Dog Biscuits are for me."*

"Fantastic!" yelled the director. "It's a

wrap! Tim, you were great! When they see this ad the world will beat a path to your door—and we'll sell a million dog biscuits. I knew you could do it!"

"That was odd," the camera operator said. "Tim's voice was great but his lips hardly moved at all."

"It doesn't matter," the director said. "No one will notice. The camera was on the dog."

"But—but—but," the bewildered actor said. "I don't think I said anything."

"Either you said it or that dog's a ventriloquist," the director laughed.

"And quite a good one too," Selby thought as he grabbed the pay packet that Mrs Trifle had forgetfully left on the counter and followed her to the car.

HIGH TIME

"That dog talks," Aunt Jetty's dreadful son, Willy, announced, pointing at Selby who was curled up on a newspaper, secretly reading it. "He talked to me last year and he tricked me into jumping into a pavlova."

"Very interesting," said Mrs Trifle, not believing a word of it and putting the pavlova she'd just made on the kitchen bench.

"I'll get him back for that," Willy said, shaking his fist.

"Now, now, Willy," Mrs Trifle said, picking up the keys to her car. "You be good to Selby while I'm out at the shops. And don't touch this pavlova. I made it for the school fete tomorrow. Just play with your toys and I'll be back in five minutes."

"My toys!" Willy said, emptying his suitcase on the carpet. "Look at this, Aunty! I have my Chief Silver Arrow bow and arrow set and my Top Cop hitting-people stick and handcuffs and my Jungle James lion net and my people-shooter catapult! I shot my brother Billy over the house and into the swimming pool with the catapult. It was really fun. Not much fun for Billy, but," Willy said. "There wasn't any water in the pool. Ha ha ha ha ha!"

"You be good," Mrs Trifle said firmly as she closed the door behind her.

"That kid has more weapons than the army," Selby thought as he ran for the back door. "Luckily his tiny brain is no match for the superior brain of a thinking, feeling dog— namely mine."

Selby slowed down for a fraction of a second and in that instant an arrow with a wire attached swished in front of him and stuck in the wall. Selby leaped forward but the wire caught him in the throat and he bounced back gasping for breath.

"Not so fast, doggie," Willy said as he closed and locked the back door. "I'm gonna make you talk."

Selby jumped to his feet and ran down the hallway towards the open bedroom window but just before he rounded the corner, Willy's lion net caught him and he crashed to the floor in a terrible tangle.

"Now then," Willy said as he clamped the handcuffs on Selby's paws and carried him back to the lounge room, "talk to Willy."

"I wouldn't talk to you if you were the last brat in the world," Selby thought. "You can even torture me and I won't talk. Gulp. *Torture?* What am I saying?"

"If you don't talk," Willy said. "I'm going to shoot you out the window with my catapult."

Selby watched as Willy put together the catapult, twisting together pieces of steel pipe and bolting it all to a wooden frame.

"The kid's a maniac!" Selby thought as he struggled to get his paws out of the handcuffs. "That thing could kill me!"

"Oh, goody goody," Willy squealed as he cranked back the giant spring. "I've always wanted to see a flying dog!"

Selby worked his paws back and forth in the handcuffs as the seat on the launching arm of the catapult came way down until it touched the floor.

"Now I'm gonna open the window," Willy said, jumping up on the kitchen bench and almost landing in Mrs Trifle's pavlova as he opened the kitchen window, "and plonk you onto the seat. Then all I have to do is pull the lever and *whissssh!*"

"Mrs Trifle should be back by now!" Selby thought as he wiggled his paws halfway out of the handcuffs. "Where is she?"

"Okay doggie," Willy said, standing between Selby and the catapult. "Last chance: talk or fly. Ha ha ha he he."

Selby's whole life flashed in front of him. He remembered when he was an ordinary little barking dog, playing on the Trifle's carpet. He remembered the moment he realised he could understand people-talk. And he remembered the day he knew he had to keep his talking a secret even if it killed him. Even if it killed him?

"No, no, not that!" he thought. "My paws are almost free. My only chance is to stall him for a second . . ."

Willy lifted Selby towards the seat.

"Okay, okay, I can talk!" Selby blurted out. "Now let me go!"

"Yiiiipppppeeeeee!" Willy screamed. "I'll let you go—right out the window!"

"But you promised you wouldn't!" Selby shouted.

"I had my fingers crossed," Willy giggled. "The joke's on you!"

Somewhere back in Selby's throat a rumbling grew to a gurgle and then a burble and a croak. His face reddened and his mouth opened and out came a blood-curdling scream that sounded something like *aaaaaaarrrrrgggggg*!

SELBY SCREAMS

Willy threw his arms up in the air at the sight of the screaming dog and fell backwards on the seat of the catapult.

What happened next is uncertain. Did Selby knock against the firing lever of the catapult as he fell? Or did he reach out and pull it when he hit the ground? Even he doesn't know. What *is* sure is that in one fleeting second, just as Mrs Trifle came in the door, Willy, with terror in his eyes, flew through the air and landed just short of the kitchen window—smack in the pavlova.

"I can't believe it!" Mrs Trifle screamed. "The kid jumped into another pavlova!"

"It's all Selby's fault," Willy bawled, wiping the pavlova out of his eyes. "He screamed at me!"

"Don't be silly," Mrs Trifle said. "Dogs can't scream."

"He did!—and he talked too!" Willy cried.

"Sorry, brat," Selby thought as he got his paws out of the handcuffs and headed off for his afternoon walk, "but nobody's ever going to believe a story like that."

BOMBS AWAY!

Slowly, as Selby watched the thirteenth and final episode of the TV show, *Inspector Quigley's Casebook* on video, he felt himself change. Now he was Inspector Selby, the super-cool detective, the quiet investigator who could tell everything about a person just from looking at their shoes, the dog who could solve the toughest crime in his tea-break. Then a faint noise woke him from his daydream.

"I do deduce," Selby said, wagging his paw in the air the way Inspector Quigley wagged his finger when he deduced something, "that that *splonk* sound was the postman—none other than Postie Paterson—leaving an article of mail on our doorstep. I further deduce," Selby went on, using his favourite Quigley-type words, "that it is a parcel for Mrs Trifle. Even without seeing it I judge the contents of said parcel to be cheesecloth for straining apples to make apple jelly. How do you know this?" he asked himself. "Simple, my dear Selby. The other day I was privy to a telephone conversation between Mrs Trifle and Health-nut Mail Order Supplies in which she ordered the cloth. I remember it well because she had to shout due to a bad telephone connection. And now I shall see if my deductive reasoning was on target," Selby said, dashing to the door and picking up a package addressed to Mrs Trifle. "Spot on," he said, feeling very proud of himself. "Hmmmmmmm. It certainly *is* heavy for a piece of cheesecloth. And there's something else that's strange—it's ticking."

Selby put the package back on the step and calmly closed the door.

"Hmmmmmmm. Ticking, eh?" he said, scratching his chin the way Inspector Quigley did. "Very curious."

Then he remembered the package that mysteriously appeared in the episode of *Inspector Quigley's Casebook* called, *The Case of the Mail Order Massacre*.

"The ever-cool Inspector Selby refuses to panic. He will not jump to the conclusion that someone has mailed a bomb to the mayor," Selby said. "What I need is one of those sniffer dogs that can smell explosives. Come to think of it maybe I *am* one of those sniffer dogs that can smell explosives."

Selby threw open the door and put his nose to the package.

"Pheeeeeeeeew! That smells awful! And what's this?" Selby said, opening and reading a note that was stuck to the package.

"'Dear customer,'" he read, "'We do hope that this doesn't go off before you receive it.' Go off? Does that really say 'go off'? Yes, indeed it does and Inspector Selby has just reached the inevitable and inescapable conclusion that this package right here before him contains an article known in detective circles as a bomb. Yikes!"

Selby slammed the door and dashed to the TV room, putting his paws over his ears.

"A bomb! A bomb on the doorstep!" he screamed. "It's about to go off! It'll blow the house to bits and me with it! I won't live to chew another Dry-Mouth Dog Biscuit! Help! Save me!"

Selby lay there for a minute wondering how to get out of the house without passing the package. Suddenly he straightened himself up.

"I can't just run away. This house is filled with all of the Trifle's valuable belongings. Not only that, the Trifles themselves might return home just before the bomb goes off. I've got to disarm it."

Selby grabbed the video tape of the Inspector Quigley episode about the bomb and fast-forwarded it to the part where the inspector told a roomful of policemen about bombs.

"The simplest thing to do with a package bomb is to smash it against the ground," Inspector Quigley told them.

"That's it!" Selby squealed as he dashed out the front door and lifted the package over his head. "Why didn't I think of it."

"The problem with this," he heard Inspector Quigley say, "is that it will probably explode if you do. All of which goes to show that the simplest answer isn't always the best answer."

"Crumbs!" Selby thought, putting the package back down.

"A direct approach is to rip open the package and get to the mechanism," the inspector continued, "and find out how it works."

"Done!" Selby said, tearing off the outer layer of paper.

"But of course some package bombs are made to go off if you do this," the inspector added. "Sometimes the direct approach isn't the best method."

"Good point," Selby said, stopping in mid-tear.

"Alternatively, you could soak it in water," Inspector Quigley said, scratching his chin. "Water will ruin a lot of explosives."

"Of course!" Selby said and he ran into the garden, grabbed the garden hose and started spraying the package.

"But, sadly," Selby heard Inspector Quigley say, "some bombs go off when they get wet and there's no real way to tell if yours will or won't."

"You've got to be kidding, Inspector!" Selby screamed, blowing furiously on the package to dry it. "Stop telling me what I *can't* do and tell me what I *can* do!"

"The fact is," the inspector said, "that anything you do to a bomb could set it off. Sometimes, running away is the only answer."

"But the house, Quig? I can't just let the house blow up," Selby thought. Then he thought again, "Oh, yes I can!"

Selby was halfway out a back window when he heard voices at the front door.

"Oh, no!" he thought. "The Trifles are back!"

"Look! This must be the cheesecloth I ordered," Mrs Trifle said, removing some of the paper from the package.

"Goodness me," Dr Trifle said, "look at the mess Postie Paterson made of it. It looks like it's been dragged through a mud puddle."

"I can't let her open it!" Selby said. "I've got to warn the Trifles even if I give away my secret forever!—even if I have to be their servant for life! I've got to *save* them."

Selby dashed into the lounge room and grabbed the package in his teeth.

"It's a bomb!" he cried in plain English, but it came out more like *hhhhuuuuuummmmmmmmbbbb* because of the package in his mouth.

"If I'm not mistaken, he wants to play toss and catch," Dr Trifle said, watching Selby hurl the package out the window.

"Speaking of mistakes," Mrs Trifle said, looking in the garden where the package had split open, spilling its contents on the grass, "those silly-billies at Healthnut didn't hear me properly. Instead of cheesecloth, they sent me some cheese and a clock—and the cheese smells like it's gone off. Phew!"

RALPHO'S MAGIC SHOW

"I don't think it was a good idea to invite Ralpho to do his show for the boy scouts and girl guides of Bogusville," Mrs Trifle said to Dr Trifle. "He's simply not a good performer. He just gets too nervous."

"Ralpho's got to learn to face an audience without going to pieces," Dr Trifle said, referring to his magician friend, Ralpho the Magnificent. "He'll never be a success as long as he gets so flustered. I just thought it would be good practice for him to entertain some very polite country children in the friendly atmosphere of our home. It'll give him confidence and the kids will love it. Besides, he says he's got something exciting to liven up his act this time."

"I'm just afraid he'll pop his cork the way he did the last time," Mrs Trifle said. "I think he was better as an inventor than as a magician. But we'll see ..."

"We *will* see," Selby thought. "I'll get to see it too. Oh boy, oh boy, I love magic shows."

And so it was that Ralpho the Magnificent arrived at the Trifle's house and set up all his magic gear just in time for the busload of children to come running into the lounge room and sit quietly on the floor. All of which would have been perfectly okay if Aunt Jetty hadn't also heard about the show. This still would have been okay if she hadn't dumped her disastrous son Barnstorm Billy outside.

"I have some errands to run," she told Billy as he ran for the Trifle's door. "You go in and have a good time. I'm sure the Trifles won't mind one more little pair of eyes and ears."

"Magician?" Billy said in a loud voice just when Ralpho was about to pull a pigeon out of a hat. "I don't want to see a stupid old magician! I thought it was a *musician*. I want to see somebody play the drums."

"You just sit there quietly, Billy," Mrs Trifle said politely. "I'm sure you'll enjoy it."

"Why oh why," Selby asked himself, "did Aunt Jetty have to bring bratty Billy? He'll spoil everything for sure."

From then on, things went terribly wrong. Ralpho pulled the pigeon out of the hat but it took one look at him and bit him on the finger. Billy burst into laughter and everyone else joined in. Then Ralpho juggled three flaming torches until he caught one by the wrong end.

"Good one, mister stupid magician man!" Billy roared as Ralpho plunged his injured fingers in a glass of water. "Was that hot enough for you?"

Now Ralpho was angry and nervous— *very* angry and nervous. But the final straw came when Ralpho's mummy broke down.

"And now," Ralpho said, putting on a turban and holding up his hands for silence, "one of the mysteries of the pyramids: the walking mummy."

Dr Trifle pulled back a curtain and there stood a mummy case covered in mummy-writing.

"Struth!" Selby thought. "This is great! Ralpho really is a good showman."

"Here in this box," Ralpho began, "is the mummy of Amen-hop-rope, a king who lived four thousand years ago. He died a terrible death when he was tricked by his slave, Tut-tut-tutmose. One day when he was quite tired of the king, the slave said, 'Oh, master of masters, you are so magnificent I'm sure you can walk on the waters of the Nile.' The king, believing his slave, stepped into the river—

and sank like a stone. He not only couldn't walk on water he also couldn't swim a stroke. Do you hear me, Amen-hop-rope?" Ralpho said and the lid of the mummy box flew open making the girls and boys gasp with delight.

"Crumbs!" thought Selby, when he saw the bandaged figure in the box. "It's fabulous! The mummy looks real!"

"It's not a real mummy and don't pretend it is!" Billy yelled out. "And you're a cheater, mister cheathead!"

"Quiet!" Ralpho said angrily, and then he turned to the mummy. "*Great* Amen-hop-rope, I Tut-tut-tutmose, say you are a fool."

As soon as Ralpho said the word *great*, the mummy's arms shot out and he started walking slowly towards Ralpho, who turned sideways and smiled at the startled children.

"Real mummies can't walk," Billy screamed. "Their legs are wrapped together!"

"Oh, yeah?" Ralpho said. "If you're so smart, tell me how it walks."

"It's got a voice-thing in it," Billy yelled. "When you say *great* it moves."

"I hate to admit it," Selby thought. "But I think Billy's right. It's a voice-activated robot. A very clever robot nevertheless."

"Quiet, kid," Ralpho said, turning quickly as the mummy was about to grab him

43

around the throat. "Oh, *wise* Amen-hop-rope," he said, "please forgive your humble slave."

The mummy dropped its arms and started back towards the box.

"You said *wise* extra loud," Billy yelled, "and that made it go back to the box."

"Did not!" Ralpho said, turning red as a beetroot.

"Did so," Billy answered. "It's a fake, mister faker! Watch this. *Great!*" Billy yelled and the mummy turned around and started back in Ralpho's direction with its arms outstretched.

"The brat is right again," Selby thought. "The robot's programmed to go one way when it hears *great* and the other way when it hears *wise*."

"*Wise!*" Ralpho yelled and the mummy turned again.

"*Great!*" yelled Billy. "It's just a robot. *Great! Great! Great!*

"*Wise! Wise! Wise!*" Ralpho screamed, bursting into tears. "Get out of here all of you! Go away! I never want to see any of you children again!"

Dr and Mrs Trifle quickly shooed the frightened girls and boys out the front door to where their bus was waiting, while Ralpho chased Billy round and round the room.

"When I catch you," Ralpho screamed, "I'm going to give you a spanking you'll never forget!"

"I'll tell!" Billy yelled back. "My mummy will spank you, mister sillyhead!"

"This is crazy," Selby thought, running for safety just as Ralpho caught Billy by the neck and started to shake him. "Ralpho's really done his lolly this time. He'll strangle the kid if someone doesn't stop him!"

"*Great! Wise! Great! Wise! Great! Wise!*" they yelled, as Amen-hop-rope turned in circles and put his arms up and down so fast that his bandages began to unwind. In a minute he was a shining silvery robot with smoke pouring from his head.

And in the heat of battle, Ralpho throttled and Billy kicked and both fell silent, not noticing that Billy had got one more *great* in and that Amen-hop-rope was walking towards them with his arms out. In a second, the robot had them both by the throat, one in each hand.

"Wiiiiii-glug-glurg!" Ralpho said, struggling to say *wise*.

"Wurg-glurg, gleeeeeeg!" Billy said, also trying to say *wise*.

"Help!" Selby thought, looking out the window where the Trifles were putting the last of the children on the bus. "If someone doesn't

45

call off the metal monster there are going to be questions asked—and Ralpho and Billy won't be doing the answering! I've got to do something!" he thought, biting Amen-hop-rope's leg and hurting his mouth in the process. "I've got to talk! My secret will be out, but I've got to do it! If only I can get to where Ralpho and Billy can't see me speak . . ."

"*Wise! Wise! Wise!*" Selby screamed.

Suddenly the robot stopped, dropped its arms and walked back to its box. The stunned Ralpho let go of Billy who tore out of the door and jumped in Aunt Jetty's car which had just driven up. Ralpho stood staring in amazement at Selby.

"I saw you talk," Ralpho said. "Very clever! Yes, very, extremely clever!"

"We're terribly sorry about everything," Dr Trifle said, as he and Mrs Trifle came in the door. "I'm afraid we didn't expect little Billy. I'm sure I can help you fix your mummy."

"Never mind the mummy! This talking dog robot you made," Ralpho said, pointing to Selby, "is a great idea! I'm going home right now to make one. It's just what I need! Bye now."

"Talking dog robots?" Mrs Trifle said, watching Ralpho drive away. "Poor Ralpho's gone completely round the twist this time."

"I don't know what he was driving at," Dr Trifle said, looking down into Selby's innocent eyes, "but I have to admit he made a better mummy robot than I could have. Maybe this dog robot is just what he needs to liven up his act."

"I don't know about livening up Ralpho's act," Selby thought. "If it got any livelier than today's, I don't think I could stand it."

A BALLOON TOO SOON

"This is fantastic!" Selby thought as the tiny dot that was Dame Cecily Quagmire's balloon appeared on the horizon. "Dame Cecily is about to be the first person to fly a balloon around the world over both the North and the South Poles, and she's stopping in Bogusville just before the end of her trip!"

Dr Trifle quickly took down the old torn flag from in front of the council chambers and replaced it with a new one as Mrs Trifle memorised her welcoming speech.

"This is an historic occasion ..." she began. "This is a truly exciting and historic occasion ... Oh, heavens," Mrs Trifle said, looking up from her notes. "I'll never get this speech right and she's nearly here."

"You could just say, 'G'day and welcome to Bogusville.'" Dr Trifle said.

"I most certainly could not," Mrs Trifle said. "Mayors aren't allowed to say 'G'day', especially when they're greeting international heroes who are making historic round-the-world, over-the-poles balloon flights."

"It was just a suggestion, dear," Dr Trifle said.

"Dame Cecily is the grand old lady of flight. She used to race aeroplanes back when they were held together with chewing gum and bailing wire. Back then they used to fly by the seat of their pants. Don't ask me how their pants helped fly the plane, but they did," Mrs Trifle said as a crowd began to gather. "These days aeroplanes are flown by computers. It seems the only things that pilots do with the seats of their pants is sit on them," she added. "By the way, why did you have to take down the old flag?"

"It was too tatty."

"Tatty or not," Mrs Trifle said, "I was sort of fond of it."

"This one's made of that special computer-designed Tare-Knot Miracle Flag Fabric," Dr Trifle said. "It should last a long time. It's so tough that you could bet your life it wouldn't tear."

Selby lay back in the shade of a tree and watched Dame Cecily's balloon come closer and closer. He remembered the last episode of the TV series *Balloon Flights of Long Ago* about the early days of ballooning.

"What a wonderful sport," he thought. "Hanging from a balloon in a big open basket. Letting the wind take you where it might. Dropping down in a meadow for a picnic lunch. Being blown off course into deserts and jungles. Being rescued by people so primitive that they've never even seen an Australian before. What a life. But wait just a minute!" Selby thought, jumping to his feet as the balloon approached. "That's no basket! It's all plastic and glass. It's like a space capsule! And it's covered in advertising!" Selby said, looking at the signs on the balloon that said FLY-RIGHT FLY SPRAY and DR POPHAM'S STONE GROUND MUESLI PELLETS and VACATION VILLA INTERNATIONAL HOTELS.

Dr Trifle grabbed a rope that hung down from the huge balloon and pulled on it until the capsule touched the ground. He tied the rope to the tree next to Selby and watched as Dame Cecily scrambled out, zipping up her flight suit and brushing her hair as she went.

"This is a . . . er . . . truly exciting and . . . um . . . historic occasion," Mrs Trifle said as a bus full of reporters drove up flashing cameras at Dame Cecily. "As the mayor of . . . um . . ."

"You're the mayor, are you dear?" Dame Cecily whispered to Mrs Trifle as she grinned

51

at the TV cameras.

"Why, yes I am," Mrs Trifle said, "and I feel deeply honoured—"

"Thank you, thank you," Dame Cecily said, grabbing a microphone. "How very nice, Mrs Mayor. But I'll make the speeches if you don't mind."

Selby put his paws up in the open doorway of the passenger capsule and peered in at the control panel.

"Ladies and gentlemen of the world," Dame Cecily said, waving her arms about. "This is a truly exciting and historic occasion. Tomorrow I will fly to Brisbane and finish the first round-the-world, over-the-poles balloon flight ever. It has been a dream of many years, a dream made possible by the kindness of Vacation Villa Hotels, who spared nothing in making me comfortable in some of the most remote corners of the world, places so primitive that the people had never even seen an Australian before. And thanks to a health-giving diet of Dr Popham's Stone Ground Muesli and thanks also to Fly-Right Fly Spray. I'd also like to thank Kevtex Wonder Fibres and Poly-carborundamide Impact-Resistant Plastics and Tru-Star Computer Navigational Aids and—

"Struth," Selby muttered as he hopped into the capsule. "Look at all this electronic gear: radios, computers, wind-speed indicators, things to make the balloon go up and things to make it go down. It's completely automatic. All Dame Cecily has to do is sit in it and tell it to go and the instruments do the thinking *and* the work."

"We are only as good as our technology. I'd like to thank Oxy-Gulp Air Supply for the system that kept me from suffocating in the stratosphere," Dame Cecily said with a laugh. "And of course many thanks to the Your-Wish-Is-My-Command Control Module which made the balloon go wherever I asked it to go."

"My goodness! She's been right up in the stratosphere! Wow!" Selby said as he turned around to hop out and his tail brushed against a row of switches, starting lights flashing, buzzers buzzing and beepers beeping. "I'd love to go straight up to the stratosphere!"

"*Your wish is my command*," an electronic voice from the control module said. "*Casting off. Casting off.*"

"Oh, no!" Selby thought as he peered out the door just in time to see the rope drop from the capsule. "Crumbs! It's taking off with me in it!"

There was a gasp from the crowd as the balloon lifted.

"I've got to get out of here fast or I'm a done dog!" Selby thought as he dived out the door of the capsule—which would have been okay if his foot hadn't caught in the seat belt that hung down outside the capsule.

"Stop that balloon!" Dame Cecily screamed as she leaped towards the dangling dog. "If that mutt finishes my round-the-world over-the-poles trip I'll lose the prize money! Help!"

"I've got to get my foot loose from this contraption!" Selby thought as the world began moving away from him. "Oh, woe woe! I'm too far up now to jump and if I fall I'm a goner!"

The balloon and the dangling Selby swept along in front of the delighted reporters, whose cameras flashed and TV cameras turned, lifting towards the top of the flagpole as it went.

"My only chance is to yell instructions to the Your-Wish-Is-My-Command Control Module. I'll just tell it to go back down," Selby thought. "But ... but ... they'll hear me. My secret will be out! The whole world will know I'm the only talking dog in Australia (and perhaps the world). I'll be put in a laboratory and scientists will ask me dumb questions from morning till night. But if I *don't* talk, I'll be dragged up and up. I'll suffocate in the stratosphere! Maybe I'll freeze to death too!"

"I command you to go down!" Selby shouted. But just as he started to speak he felt the curious feeling of Tare-Knot Miracle Flag Fabric flapping against his mouth and making what he said come out more like, "Iicabubbutubugobodonnnn!" the way it would if you tried to say "I command you to go down" with a flag flapping against your mouth.

"It's the new flag!" Selby thought as he

lunged at it and grabbed a corner in his mouth. "My only hope is to hold on tight and pray the flag doesn't rip!"

"Look! He's holding the flag with his teeth!" Mrs Trifle yelled at Dr Trifle. "Climb the flagpole and rescue him before the balloon pulls him away!"

"I have a better idea," said Dr Trifle, who wasn't much good at climbing flagpoles. "I'll just lower the flag in the usual way," he added, pulling on one of the flag ropes. "That should pull Selby down along with the balloon."

"Don't just talk about it!" Selby thought, as he felt the flag slipping between his teeth. "Blinkin' well do it!"

Cameras whirred and clicked and reporters screeched into microphones as Dr Trifle lowered the flag and grasped Selby and the dangling seat belt under one arm. A crowd rushed forward and grabbed Dame Cecily's balloon.

"If I didn't know better," Dame Cecily said, as she helped lash the balloon to the flagpole, "I'd swear that dog was talking. Come to think of that, how did he get the balloon to go up?"

"You see I told you that you could bet your life that Tare-Knot Miracle Flag Fabric wouldn't tear," Dr Trifle said to Mrs Trifle as he prised the flag from Selby's trembling mouth.

"You were right," Selby thought as he barged past Dame Cecily on his way home to watch another episode of *Balloon Flights of Long Ago*. "But it wasn't your life that was bet—it was mine!"

Nose Business Like Snow Business

"Yahoooooo! It's my turn in a couple of minutes," "Head-Plant" Hemholtz shouted as he looked out the window of his ski chalet at skiers jumping off the ski-jump in the annual Twisted Skis Ski-Jumping Championship. "This is my chance to win the championship at last. I've always wanted that Golden Twisted Skis Trophy. Grab your parkas, Dr and Mrs Trifle, and follow me. Just watch my technique!"

"I'm afraid that when it comes to technique, Head-Plant doesn't have very much," Dr Trifle said as the skier raced towards the ski-jump. "If he'd only land on his feet, I'm sure there would be a big improvement. Do you know that the only time he ever landed on his feet, he skidded off the slope and right into the back of an ambulance?"

NOSE BUSINESS LIKE SNOW BUSINESS

"At least he got to hospital very quickly that time," Mrs Trifle said as she buckled up her boots. "Poor HP. It's very kind of him to let us stay in his chalet but it's not much fun watching him break all his bones every year in the Twisted Skis Championship. Sometimes I wonder if he has the foggiest notion what he's doing."

Selby was about to follow the Trifles out into the snow when Dr Trifle turned in the doorway and stopped him.

"I'm sorry, Selby, old bean," he said, not thinking for a minute that Selby could understand everything he was saying, "but your fur just isn't thick enough for this cold. You'd better stay inside where it's warm."

"It's not fair," Selby thought as he watched Dr and Mrs Trifle struggle through the snow towards the ski-jump. "They bring me all the way to the Twisted Skis Ski-Jumping Championship and now they won't let me watch. Last year I only knew Head-Plant had jumped when I heard the ambulance taking him to hospital. If only I had some warm clothing I could go out there without freezing. I'd only have to be careful that no one saw me. Why doesn't anyone make ski parkas for dogs? But wait! I think I've got it!"

Selby raced to a wardrobe and got out

stacks and stacks of cold-weather clothing. He pulled on a child's parka, putting his front legs through the sleeves. Then he put on another one upside down with his hind legs poking out the sleeves.

"I may look like two midgets in a spacesuit," Selby thought as he put on one of the parka hoods and let the other dangle between his legs, "but in all this blowing snow, no one will notice me and I can watch the ski-jumping without worrying about freezing to death."

Selby stood in the crowd at the bottom of the ski-jump but it was snowing so heavily that he could hardly see a thing. The ski-jumpers were just blurs in the air until they touched down on the ski slope nearby.

"I think I'd rather watch them start down the jump than land. I'd better go up to the top," Selby thought as he started up the ski-jump stairs. "That way I won't have to see Head-Plant's yearly catastrophe. I do hate the sight of blood and gore. Uh-oh, here he goes now."

"Ladies and gentlemen," the announcer said over the loudspeaker, "the final skier, Head-Plant Hemholtz, is about to jump. Anyone at the bottom of the jump, please move back so he doesn't land on you. And please don't watch unless you like blood and gore."

Selby arrived at the top of the ski-jump and stood just above Head-Plant as the skier was about to begin his run.

"All right!" he heard Head-Plant say. "Just tell me when I can go. I just can't wait to be sailing through the air. It's such a great feeling. I'm not so keen on landing but."

"I've got a perfect view!" Selby thought as he felt his feet go into a slow slide, bringing him straight down the runway towards Head-Plant. "Yiiiiiiikes!"

"Yiiiiikes! What's that sliding towards me? It looks like two midgets in a spacesuit!" Head-Plant yelled as he shot off down the ski-jump with Selby sliding after him. "I'd better get out of here before it knocks me over."

"Heeeeeeeeeeelp!" Selby screamed as he skidded on all fours, gaining on Head-Plant and looking around for something to grab hold of. "I'm going off a ski-jump without any skis! Somebody stop me! I'm sure it's against the law!"

Just at the lip of the ski-jump Head-Plant crouched down and was about to give an extra big jump when Selby grabbed the seat of the skier's pants in his teeth—banging his nose in the process—and the two of them went flying head-over-skis through the air.

"Not a bad take-off," said Head-Plant,

who always went head-over-skis through the air when he went off a ski-jump, "but I wish this thing would let go of my trousers!"

"Oh, noooooo!" Selby thought. "The silly man doesn't even know he's supposed to keep his head up and his skis down! Even I know that, and I don't know how to ski! I've got to do something fast or we'll both land in hospital! I'll just have to tell him what to do!"

"All right, Head-Plant," Selby said through his teeth "just do exactly as I say and everything will be okay!"

"Wait a minute! Who are you and who do you think is doing the skiing here?" Head-Plant cried.

"Certainly not you!" Selby yelled as they tumbled over again and again. "Now straighten yourself up and put your arms down at your sides the way the other ski-jumpers do!"

"Hmmmm," Head-Plant said, straightening up and putting his arms down. "What an interesting idea. Why didn't I think of that?"

"Never mind about that! Now put your skis together!" Selby shouted, pushing the skis together. "And point them up at a forty-five degree angle."

"I don't know anything about angles," Head-Plant said, pointing his skis in the air, "but how's this?"

"It'll have to do!" Selby yelled, wiping the snow from his eyes.

Dr and Mrs Trifle watched as a big blue blur with a smaller blur, that looked like two midgets in a spacesuit sailed past them towards the bottom of the slope.

"That can't be Head-Plant," Dr Trifle

said, peeping through his fingers at the beautiful landing. "He's actually landed on his feet."

"I did it! I did it!" Head-Plant yelled. "Now how do you stop these things?"

"I'm afraid it is Head-Plant," Mrs Trifle said to Dr Trifle as Head-Plant skied straight through the crowd and crashed into the window of his own chalet. "I'd recognise that technique anywhere."

The Trifles and the ambulance attendants raced forward, dragged the injured skier from the wreckage and put him on a stretcher.

"Head-Plant!" Mrs Trifle cried. "Are you alive? Can you hear me?"

"Of course I can hear you," Head-Plant said, as they carried him off towards the ambulance. "Have I won the Golden Twisted Skis?"

"Just barely," Dr Trifle answered. "I just heard the announcer. It seems you won it by a nose."

"What they'll never know," Selby thought as he whipped off the ski gear and crawled out of the wreckage rubbing his sore nose, "is that it was *my* nose he won it by."

SELBY SHAKEN

"Earthquake!" Mrs Trifle screamed as she jumped straight over Selby and out the window, landing in some bushes next to where Dr Trifle was clearing away some sticks and rocks.

"Good heavens!" Dr Trifle said. "Are you quite all right?"

"Didn't you feel that earthquake?" Mrs Trifle cried. "It was just as Professor Rumblecrumble said on TV last night. It felt like a huge truck rumbling along a bumpy street."

"The only thing I felt," Dr Trifle said as he helped his wife out of the bushes, "was the council garbage truck rumbling along our street."

"So it *was* a truck. How embarrassing," Mrs Trifle said, turning quite pink. "I wish I hadn't watched *Great Earthquakes of the World*. It's got me so nervous. I just can't stop thinking about the earth cracking and houses falling down and all that awful business."

"An earthquake could never happen here in Bogusville," Dr Trifle (who hadn't watched *Great Earthquakes of the World*) said. "Stop worrying."

"I wish there was something to take my mind off earthquakes," Mrs Trifle said with a sigh. "Something soothing."

"I've got just what you need. Tonight *The Screaming Mimis* are making a recording at the Bijou Theatre," Dr Trifle said, referring to the famous pop supergroup. "Apparently they need an audience to help make some noises."

Inside the house, Selby (who *had* seen *Great Earthquakes of the World*) and who would have jumped out the window too if he hadn't been too busy searching for a pesky flea to notice the rumbling, pricked up his ears.

"Noises is right," Mrs Trifle said. "They make more noise than a jumbo jet. I'm sure I wouldn't enjoy it."

"She has a point," Selby thought as he remembered the time he got stuck in the *Mimis'* Computerised High-Pitched Ear-Piercing Brain-Scrambling Blaster during one of their rock concerts.

"They're not using their Computerised High-Pitched Brain-Scrambling Blaster," Dr Trifle said. "They're only making soothing noises now."

"Are you quite sure?" Mrs Trifle asked.

"Apparently they're making a whole record with songs about nature. It's going to be called *Earthsongs*. They need people to babble like brooks and whistle like the wind apparently. It should be quite soothing music."

"What sort of people do they need?"

"Clever people like us, I should imagine."

"I can't believe it!" Selby thought. "My favourite pop supergroup, *The Screaming Mimis*, making a record! That Mimi is so great! I just must see her perform, even if I have to sneak in."

When Dr and Mrs Trifle arrived at the theatre that night they saw half of Bogusville seated in the audience. What they didn't see as they took their seats was Selby creeping in behind them and hiding under Mrs Trifle's seat.

"That's her! That's Mimi!" Selby thought as he peered out through a forest of legs towards the stage. "I can't wait to hear these nature songs." He nibbled the fur of his leg, searching for the flea that had been biting him all day.

"You're probably wondering what all this is about," Mimi said into the microphone. "Well we're making a concept album called *Earthsongs* and we needed some very ordinary people like yourselves to help out. Each song on the record is about a natural disaster like a cyclone or a rockslide or a tidal wave or a volcano exploding. What we want you to do is whistle, break sticks, bang rocks together and stuff like that. We'll pass around all the necessary materials when the time comes. Got the picture?"

"Oh boy, oh boy, oh boy!" Selby thought. "She's so terrific! Even the way she holds the microphone is exciting."

"While I sing and play the Scream-o-phone," Mimi continued, "Slam-Bam Benson here will play the Wobble-board and the Explosion-simulator. Okay?"

"Scream-o-phone? Wobble-board? Explosion-simulator? It doesn't sound very soothing," Mrs Trifle whispered to Dr Trifle.

"At least it should take your mind off earthquakes," Dr Trifle answered.

For three hours, *The Screaming Mimis* recorded each song over and over to get the sounds just the way they wanted them. The audience whistled till their lips were cracked, roared till their throats were sore, banged rocks together till their fingers tingled and screamed themselves silly.

"I'm exhausted," Dr Trifle said to Mrs Trifle. "All this rock and stick business is more tiring than gardening. What sort of music do you think they call this?"

"I'm really not sure that it's music at all," Mrs Trifle said in a raspy voice. "Doesn't music have to have notes in it?"

"I don't know if it's music either," Selby thought as he lay back on one elbow, "but I haven't had such a good time for years."

"Please sit down!" Mimi yelled as some of the audience started to leave. "We've got one more song to do. If we don't finish this one, we don't have a record. Okay, now which one are we going to do, Slam?" she asked Slam-Bam.

"This one's called 'Earthpeace'," Slam-Bam said. "It's a quiet one."

"Oh, Slam," Mimi said. "Not a quiet one. That's no fun. Can't we do another disaster track?"

"No we can't!" Slam-Bam boomed. "This one's supposed to sound like the calm after the storm. You agreed."

"Okay, okay, keep your shirt on," Mimi said, then turned to the audience. "Now listen carefully. We only have enough tape for one take so we've got to make this one count. No mistakes. It's simple. All you have to do is some gentle blowing, like a breeze in the trees, and the whistling of birds. Okay, ready, set, go!"

Selby was just puckering up to add to the breeze noise when he felt the flea he'd been after all day on the back of his front leg and began scratching furiously with his hind paw. All of which would have been okay if his leg hadn't pounded the floor making a thumping noise that sounded sort of like a truck rumbling along a bumpy street.

"Hey! Who's doing that?" Mimi screamed. "Stop it right now! It's ruining the song!"

Just then something in Mrs Trifle's brain

snapped. "It's an earthquake!" she cried. "Earthquake!"

All through the audience (all of whom had seen *Great Earthquakes of the World* the night before), brains snapped like breaking sticks. Suddenly there were screams of "Earthquake!" and "Help!" and "Save us!" and other things that you can't write in a book like this, and they thundered out of the theatre leaving the stunned Mimi standing on stage.

"It's all my fault!" Selby thought as he crept along an empty aisle towards a side window. "I started a stampede! I ruined the record! Mimi will never come back to Bogusville again. This is a *real* disaster!"

"That was great!" Mimi suddenly yelled to Slam-Bam. "It sounded just like a mob of simple villagers fleeing an earthquake."

"That's just what it was: the simple villagers of Bogusville fleeing an earthquake," Slam-Bam said. "We can call it, 'Villagers Fleeing'. Now let's get out of this dump and back to civilisation before there's another earthquake."

"A better title would be," Selby thought as he headed for home, "'Selby De-Fleaing'."

THE MUMMY'S CURSE

"I just bought this mummy and I'm very excited about it," said Professor Krakpott when Dr Trifle and Selby visited him at the Department of Old and Crusty Things at the Federal University, "but I can't quite figure out the writing on the ancient mummy case. I thought you could give me a hand."

Dr Trifle put on his glasses to see the writing that was painted on the lid of the mummy case which lay on the floor of the room.

"I'd be happy to help," he said, "but I've forgotten all the ancient mummy writing I ever knew."

"That's a pity," Professor Krakpott said, "but I'm sure, between the two of us, we'll work out what it says."

"Who sold it to you?"

"One of those mummy dealers who goes crawling around in ancient tombs wearing a sheet around him and a turban on his head. Trevor's his name."

"Trevor?" Dr Trifle said.

Selby looked around the dusty old storeroom.

"Sheeeesh!" he thought as a shiver went up his spine. "How can Professor Krakpott work here surrounded by mummies? I'd be looking over my shoulder every two seconds just to make sure that none of them was creeping up behind me. Ralpho's robot mummy was bad enough."

"Trevor brought it in about an hour ago. I paid him $50,000," Professor Krakpott said. "I think it was well worth it, the writing's so clear it could have been painted this morning. He said he'd give me a hundred dollars back as a special Mummy's Day discount."

"He has a sense of humour, this Trevor," Dr Trifle said.

"Yes, but I do believe he forgot to give me the hundred dollars back because after I handed him the $50,000 I turned to do something and when I turned back—he was gone. It was all very odd."

"Very odd indeed," Dr Trifle agreed. "Did he tell you anything about the mummy?"

"He warned me that there's an ancient curse on it."

"What sort of ancient curse?"

"The sort that says that if anyone opens the box and sets eyes on the mummy they'll die."

"You mean you bought a mummy and now you can't even open the case to look at it because you might die?"

"That's right, but frankly I never believe a word Trevor says," Professor Krakpott said. "He's a bit . . . well, unreliable when it comes to the facts. I wouldn't be surprised if he was completely wrong about the curse."

"You mean he's a liar."

"Well, yes," Professor Krakpott said, "but after he'd gone I discovered some writing on the top of the case that worried me. It seems to say, 'Beware! Do not open this case, you funny cup', or something of the sort. That could be the curse that Trevor tried to warn me about."

"'You funny cup'?" Dr Trifle said. "Are you sure it says that?"

"Well it might say, 'you simple glass'," Professor Krakpott said. "Either way I thought I'd better make sure I know exactly what it means before we open the case."

"Before *we* open the case?" Dr Trifle asked.

"Of course. Now let's go and look it up in

a copy of the *Dictionary of Ancient Mummy Writing*. There's one in the library."

"You stay here, Selby," Dr Trifle said and he and Professor Krakpott hurried out of the storeroom, closing the door behind them.

"Oh, no!" Selby thought. "I'm trapped in a room full of mummies! I can't turn the knob and open the door because, if I do, they'll suspect I'm not an ordinary dog. This is awful! Even my worst nightmares aren't this bad! I've just got to keep from panicking till Dr Trifle and the professor come back and open the door."

Selby whistled every tune he could think of including the ones from every commercial he'd seen in the past five years. In a few minutes, his mouth was as dry as a desert and he'd run out of tunes.

"It's okay. Everything's okay," he said to himself. "Nothing's going to happen. Dr Trifle and the professor will be back soon and then everything will be all right. I'm sure everything's going to be all right."

Selby moved forward to the new mummy case and studied the ancient mummy writing on the lid.

"Hmmmmmm," he thought. "The professor was right. It's so fresh and bright that it could have been painted this morning."

Suddenly Selby heard a *tap* and then another *tap* followed by a couple of *thumps*. Suddenly the lid began to rise in front of his nose.

"Wha-what's this?" he thought. "What's happening? It's as though the m-mummy's trying to get out of the case. It can't be! That mummy's been d-dead for thousands of years!"

Selby watched as the lid of the mummy case rose higher and higher. Try as he did to

stay calm, his heart was pounding in his chest and sweat poured down his forehead.

"I've got to stay perfectly quiet!" Selby thought as a noise rumbled within him, a noise that came up and up until it came out in a huge scream that sounded something like, "Aggggggggggghhhhhhhhhh!" and was so loud that it shook the dust from the rafters.

The lid dropped back down and Selby tore into a corner and hid. Then it began to rise again.

"It's alive!" Selby screamed in plain English. "It's going to get me! The curse says that if I even look at it I'll die!"

Selby watched as the mummy's bandaged head began to come out of the case.

"What am I going to do?" Selby thought as he put a paw over his eyes so he wouldn't see the mummy. "If I race for the door, I'll see the mummy and die! If I stand here with my paw over my eyes, he'll get me for sure! I've got to think of something fast! I've got it!" he thought. "It's my only chance! I'll have to keep the mummy from coming out!"

Selby made a great leap into the air and landed squarely on the lid, knocking the bandaged head back down. He put his paws around the case to hold it closed.

"Let me out of here!" the voice in the case yelled.

"Not on your life!" Selby yelled back. "Or mine, for that matter!"

"I'll tell you what," the voice said, "let's

make a deal."

"'Let's make a deal'? That doesn't sound like mummy-talk," Selby thought as he suddenly realised that the bandaged head of the mummy was really the turbaned head of none other than Trevor the mummy dealer who had hidden in the mummy case to avoid paying the professor his hundred dollar Mummy's Day discount he'd promised him.

"Let me out of here, I beg you!" the voice said.

With his nose pressed tight against the lid of the mummy case, Selby smelled something strange.

"Hey, what's this?" Selby thought. "This paint's still wet. This ancient writing was only painted this morning."

"I know it's you in there, Trevor," Selby said, imitating the professor's voice. "This is Professor Krakpott and you just cheated me out of $50,000 *and* the Mummy's Day discount."

"Just let me out and I promise I'll never do it again," Trevor pleaded.

"Not good enough," Selby said. "You have to promise to give the money back straight away."

"Scout's honour," Trevor said.

"Now wait a minute!" Selby thought.

"What am I saying? If I let him out of here he'll see I'm not the professor after all. He'll see that it's me, Selby, a talking dog. My secret will be out. There's no telling what a conniving mummy dealer might do if he found a talking dog. I might be sold into slavery. But I'm stuck, I can't let him out and I can't let Dr Trifle and Professor Krakpott see me holding the lid down like this or they'll know I'm not an ordinary not-so-dumb animal."

Just then Selby heard the storeroom door begin to open.

"Oh, no! What am I going to do," he thought, and in a second he did the only thing he could: jumped off the case and curled up on the ground as if nothing had happened.

And as soon as the door was open, Trevor jumped out of the mummy case and dashed past Dr Trifle and Professor Krakpott.

"Okay, you win," he yelled at the professor. "You can keep the money!"

"How very strange," Professor Krakpott said. "That was Trevor. What money do you think he was referring to?"

"I have no idea," Dr Trifle said. "It seems to me that *he* kept all the money."

"Look! The case is open!" Professor Krakpott said. "And it's empty. I've been diddled by that devilish dealer! It's an ancient case but without the ancient mummy that was once inside. Knowing him, he's sold me the empty case and sold the mummy to someone else."

"There may not be a mummy in it but there seems to be plenty of *money*," Dr Trifle said, picking the $50,000 out of the mummy case. "I think his conscience got the better of him and he gave it all back."

"And look at this writing," the professor said, closing the lid again to read it. "Just as I thought. It doesn't say, 'Do not open this case, you funny cup'. It says, 'Do not open this case, you silly mug'. I wonder what that means?"

"If you don't know," Selby thought as he trotted out through the open door, "I'm certainly not going to tell you."

THE BEAST OF BOGUSVILLE

Mrs Trifle slammed down the phone in a panic. "There's still no sign of Postie Paterson," she said to Dr Trifle. "He finished at the post office at ten o'clock and now he's gone. He was going to the zoo to fix Tina the tiger's cage but now he's completely vanished —disappeared off the face of the earth."

Selby's ears pricked up.

"That's spooky," he thought as a tingle of fear went through his body. "Imagine someone just disappearing off the face of the earth."

"There are rumours floating around," Mrs Trifle continued.

"What sort of rumours?" Dr Trifle asked as he turned on the radio and began searching for his favourite program.

"Strange ones. Melanie Mildew said he could have hit his head and forgotten who he was and then caught the bus to Melbourne."

"*That is* strange. There aren't any buses

from Bogusville to Melbourne."

"I didn't believe it either," Mrs Trifle said. "Phil Philpot said that Postie might have been kidnapped by martians."

"Very unlikely," Dr Trifle said, twiddling the knobs on the radio. "The problem with people is they're just not logical. When someone vanishes there's always a simple explanation."

"So what's the simple explanation here?"

"Tina ate him."

"Don't joke. Tina loves Postie. She wouldn't do anything to hurt him," Mrs Trifle said. "When he finished at the zoo he was going to the cemetery to clean some mud out of a drain. But no one's heard from him since. I'm worried."

"We can't look for him now, it's after dark," Dr Trifle said, putting on his sensible voice. "I'm sure he'll show up. If he doesn't, we'll go looking in the morning. Shhhhhhh, Tim Trembly's *Tales of Terror* is about to begin. Sit down and relax."

"How can anyone relax when they're listening to *Tales of Terror*?" Selby thought as Tim started telling his weekly horror story. "It's so scary."

"There was a time when eerie shadows crept," Tim said in his special quivery voice.

"There was a time when little babies wept. There was a time when the night wind howled and creatures scurried to the safety of their dens. There was a time, there was a time when the moonlight flowed like icy dragon's blood through the streets of a tiny Australian town."

"Gulp," Selby said as he felt the fur on his back stand up. "'Flowed like icy dragon's blood'. That's really spooky. Tim Trembly really knows how to make a story spooky."

"There was a time when the chill wind raked the trees with a thousand fingers," Tim continued. "When shutters banged and windows slammed and doors were bolted. When frightened people shivered in their beds. Suddenly a lone bat flew and a pale cloud knifed its way across the silvery surface of the moon casting the town into darkness. The time was midnight," Tim Trembly said in a loud whisper, "and the bell in the old steeple went *clong clong clong*, crying a warning to every living soul."

"I wish Tim wasn't so good at telling stories," Selby thought, suddenly noticing that his leg had gone to sleep. "It's just too frightening."

"And then the slimy beast crept from the churchyard to walk the deserted streets howling, *aroooooooooooooooooooo!* Searching for the blood of its next victim."

"'Searching for the blood of its next victim'—sheeeesh!" Selby thought. "I can't take much more of this."

"Just then there was a *knock knock knock* at a door," Tim continued, "followed by the sound of splintering wood as the beast ripped the old door from its hinges. He stepped into the darkened hallway, panting and drooling."

"Right, that's it," Selby thought, spying an open door and limping towards it. "I don't have to take this. I'm going for a nice walk."

Selby walked through deserted streets, trying to get the pins and needles out of his leg.

"Slimy beast. Terror stalking the streets. How can anyone as logical as Dr Trifle listen to that rubbish?" Selby thought, suddenly wondering what had happened to Postie Paterson.

Selby hobbled along until he saw the black outline of the church steeple ahead and the high walls of the cemetery beside it.

"It's so silly," Selby said. "Two minutes of that silly program and now I won't be able to sleep for a week."

As he passed the church, the bells in the steeple rang out with a *clong* and a *clong* and some more *clongs*. Then a cat scurried to safety and a lone bat flew over.

"Crumbs," he mumbled, still trying to

get his leg working as a pale cloud knifed its way across the silvery surface of the moon. "This is sort of like the story. Maybe—no, what am I thinking? There are no such things as slimy beasts. And as for cemeteries, I don't know why we're scared of them. They're such peaceful places, full of trees and flowers. Why, I've written some of my best poems right here in this one, lying by that big tree over there," he added as he looked up into the darkened branches nearby. "I can't let my fear get the better of me. I'll just go in there and prove that it's perfectly okay."

Selby squeezed through the rusty iron gate and sat in a cool clump of weeds.

"There. Nothing to fear," he thought. "I can even feel a poem coming on. Let's see now:

"O lovely cemetery
What makes you seem so scary?
With grass and graves and other charms
I welcome you with open arms,"

Selby said, stretching out his front paws as if to welcome the misty darkness around him.

"Not bad but I'll have to work on it more later. Hmmmmmm. I wonder what *did* happen to Postie? Whatever it was, I'm sure Dr Trifle's right. No matter how weird something seems, there's always a logical explanation."

Suddenly the clouds parted and a huge dark figure climbed out of a hole right next to Selby.

"Uh-oh! What's that?" Selby thought as the figure moved closer and a chill wind raked the trees with a thousand fingers. "Whatever it is, I'm s-s-sure there's a l-logical explanation for it."

"Owwwwww!" the figure howled, the moon glistening on its slimy surface.

"I m-may not *know* what the l-logical explanation is," Selby said, struggling against some weeds that were wrapped around his foot, "but I'm s-sure there is one."

"Owwwwww!" the figure screamed again and Selby saw the glistening face, twisted with pain.

"I t-think I may just t-trot along home," Selby thought as he madly bit at the weeds, "and m-make an early n-night of it."

Selby tore himself free and darted through the old gate, only to see the hulking figure throw itself over the high wall and land on the roadway behind him.

"Owwwwww!" it howled again and its feet squished along the wet road. "Owwwwww!"

"M-m-maybe if I really t-think hard," Selby thought as he hobbled away, just ahead

of the slimy figure, "I'll come up with the l-logical explanation for this."

"Owwwwwwwwwwwww!" the creature howled again.

"Crumbs! And d-double crumbs!" Selby mumbled as he sped up only to find the figure so close behind that each swish of his tail touched its knees. "I w-wish I could get my leg w-working properly."

A light rain began to fall as the figure lurched along, each step bringing it closer to the panting Selby.

"I'm (pant) thinking (pant) as logically as I can," Selby thought as he struggled along Bunya-Bunya Crescent and then turned into the Trifle's driveway, "but the only (pant) thing I can think of is that this (pant) slimy beast is after the blood of its next victim—(gulp) my blood! Oh, no! Someone's closed the door! (pant) How am I going to (pant) get away from him! I can feel his breath on my back! I've got to get in the house!"

Selby took a running leap, throwing himself against the door, and he bounced off straight into a pair of slimy hands that clutched him tight around the middle.

"This is it! I'm a done dog!" Selby thought. "I've got to call the Trifles! My secret doesn't matter now!"

Suddenly the front door flew open and the horrified Trifles stood stock still staring at the dark figure.

"Help! Save me from the slimy beast!" were the words on the tip of Selby's tongue when all at once a smile spread across Mrs Trifle's face.

"Postie!" she cried as she watched the mud streak down his soggy clothing. "It's you! What happened?"

"I'm afraid I took longer to clean the mud out of that drain than I expected," he said with a gasp. "And then I fell right into it and hurt my leg. Owwwwww!"

"Let's have a look at it," Dr Trifle, who knew nothing about hurt legs, said.

"It'll be okay. It's just a bit painful. You'd better have a look at Selby here. I think he *does* have a hurt leg," Postie said, handing Selby to Dr Trifle. "I'd better go home and get cleaned up."

"Didn't I tell you there's a logical explanation for everything?" Dr Trifle said when the postman had gone. "I'm sure we'd all be better off if we thought logically."

"I'm sure we would, dear," Mrs Trifle said, looking at Selby's leg and finding nothing wrong with it.

"Logical, schmogical," Selby thought as he heard the music that ended Tim Trembly's *Tales of Terror*. "One more second and you'd have heard a dog screaming for help in plain English. I'd like to see you explain that one logically."

THE AWFUL TRUTH

"I wish people would be more helpful," Mrs Trifle said with a sigh. "I asked the people of Bogusville for ideas on how to keep the town's expenses down and no one gave any. No one cares. What's worse, there's been a rash of stealing."

"What's gone missing?" Dr Trifle asked, as he poured some liquid into a bottle.

"Light globes," Mrs Trifle said. "They're being taken from streetlights and even from the council chambers."

"This could be the answer," Dr Trifle said, swirling the funny-smelling chemical around. "It's a new invention of mine called *Blabbo*."

"If Blabbo is the answer," Mrs Trifle said. "What is the question?"

"You don't understand. My Blabbo is really the not-very-well-known chemical, di-ethyl-tri-beryl-poly-wanna-kraka."

"All that in a little jar?"

"It's a new kind of truth serum."

"Truth serum?" thought Selby, who was nibbling a Dry-Mouth Dog Biscuit. "Dr Trifle's gone bonkers this time."

"You mean people drink that and they have to tell the truth?"

"Exactly. When the police catch a suspect, all they have to do is give him—or her," the doctor added to be polite, "one sip and he—or she—won't be able to lie to save their lives. It lasts for about an hour and then wears off."

"Have you taken some yourself?"

"I would have taken some myself but I only ever tell the truth anyway. So it wouldn't be much good, would it?" Dr Trifle said, blushing from ear to ear. "I'm sure it'll work. I've given some to the police to use on their next suspect."

Suddenly the telephone rang.

Mrs Trifle picked it up. "Yes? Yes? Yes? No. Yes. No!" she said, the way people do when they talk on the phone. "I'll be there in a jiffy," she added, putting down the receiver.

"What is it, dear?" Dr Trifle asked. "You look like you've seen a ghost."

"That was Sergeant Short. It seems that my sister, Jetty, has just been caught sneaking into the council chambers with a ladder under one arm."

"You mean—?"

"Yes. He thinks she's the globe grabber. Hurry! We've got to go to the town hall straight away. I can't believe it! My own sister, a criminal! The family honour will be in tatters! I'll never be able to show my face again."

"Don't jump to conclusions. She could be completely innocent," said Dr Trifle, also jumping to the conclusion that Aunt Jetty was guilty and jumping into the car with Mrs Trifle and Selby. "The police will try out my Blabbo. We should know if she's guilty soon."

"Are you sure your Blabbo is safe?" Mrs Trifle asked as they tore through the darkened town.

"When scientists think a new medicine is safe," Dr Trifle said, "they try it out on animals just to be sure. So that's what I did and so far it's okay."

"You mean you gave some to a poor unsuspecting animal?"

"Yes, so your poor unsuspecting sister should be quite okay."

"Hmmmmmmmmm," Selby thought as he munched on a bit of dog biscuit that had been stuck in his teeth. "I wonder what sort of poor unsuspecting animal Dr Trifle tried it out on."

"What sort of poor unsuspecting animal

did you try it out on?" Mrs Trifle asked.

"I put some on Selby's dog biscuits," Dr Trifle said, "and he seems to be okay—well at least so far."

"Oh, no!" Selby thought, suddenly noticing the warm feeling of the truth serum in his stomach. "Dr Trifle's tricked me into testing his Blabbo! It's not fair! He's turned me into his guinea pig!"

The car skidded to a stop in front of the town hall and the Trifles dashed inside. There, lying on the floor of the council chambers, was the whole of Bogusville's police force, Sergeant Short and Constable Long. Standing over them with her arms folded was Aunt Jetty.

"Jetty! What have you done to these poor men?" Mrs Trifle shrieked at her sister.

"I didn't lay a hand on them!" Aunt Jetty protested. "They wanted me to take some truth serum and I said no way, not till *they* took some first. So they did, and that's when the fighting began."

Sergeant Short staggered to his feet and pulled Constable Long up by his shirt.

"What did you say about my haircut, you big-nosed beanpole?" he demanded.

"I said you looked like you lost a fight with a lawn-mower," Constable Long answered. "You asked for the truth and you got it!"

"That's the last time you'll make a nasty crack about my hair!" Sergeant Short said, giving the constable a good shake. "I'll have you fired for insulting a superior officer."

"Hah! Talk about insults! What did you say about my nose?"

"I only said it was big. Big is big, there's no getting around it. You asked a question and I gave a truthful answer."

"Gentlemen! Stop it!" Mrs Trifle said. "Stop telling the truth about each other this instant. It's only causing problems."

"But we can't help it," Constable Long said. "That beryl-meryl-whatsis won't let us tell even the most innocent lies."

"All right, sister," Mrs Trifle said, turning to Jetty, "did you or did you not steal those light globes?"

"Me? Steal?" Aunt Jetty said innocently. "I'm as honest as the day is long."

"If you're so honest," Dr Trifle said, thinking of what a short day it had been, "why were you caught skulking about in the town hall with a ladder?"

"I was removing light globes," Aunt Jetty said flatly.

"So it is true!" Mrs Trifle exclaimed. "You were *stealing* light globes."

"Not so fast, sis. *Removing* is not *stealing*.

You wanted to save some of the rate-payers'
money in this stupid little town and I simply
helped. It obviously took a clever person like
me from out of town to come up with the
idea."

"Will you tell us how, exactly, you expected to save Bogusville money?" Mrs Trifle
asked. "It'll cost us a fortune to replace all
those light globes."

"You won't have to replace them. They're
right here," Aunt Jetty said, opening a closet
door and letting out a flood of globes. "Think
of what you've been saving on your electricity
bill."

"Electricity bill?" Dr Trifle asked.

"Sure. With the globes out it'll save electricity," Aunt Jetty said. "You see, I'm no more a crook than that silly dog of yours. You're not a crook are you?" she added, poking Selby with her walking-stick.

"Oh, no!" Selby thought, and panic spread through his body. "She just asked me a question and now I *have* to answer it! The truth serum won't let me *not* answer! Help! I have to tell the truth and the truth will ruin me because everyone will know I'm a talking, feeling dog—the only one in Australia and perhaps the world! At first they'll be delighted. I'll have long conversations with the Trifles in front of a roaring fire. We'll talk about things so interesting that I'll go to sleep happy every night. Sure, that's what'll happen at first—but then what? Then it'll be, 'Selby, dear, would you mind answering the telephone while we're out?' and 'Would you please pop down to the shops to get a few things for dinner?' and 'How about mowing the lawn?' *How about mowing the lawn!* How soon they forget to say 'please'! I can't answer. I can't. But I have to ..."

Selby stepped forward and was about to say, "You know perfectly well I'm not a crook," when Mrs Trifle spoke for him.

"You know perfectly well he's not a

crook. He's only a wonderful little dog," she said, picking up the relieved Selby and giving him a big hug. "Now let's go home before I tell the truth about what I think of you, Jetty."

"Phew! That was close," Selby thought. "Now I'll just have to keep my toes crossed that nobody asks me any more questions till the truth serum wears off."

BEATING AROUND THE BUSH

"This is hopeless," Dr Trifle said to Mrs Trifle as he cut another branch off a tall bush and sent it tumbling down next to Selby who was trying to find some shade. "It just doesn't look like what it's supposed to be."

"It looks like a bush, dear," said Mrs Trifle, who was too busy worrying about what to do with Dudley Dewmop, Bogusville's short-sighted part-time dog catcher, to notice what her husband was doing.

"It's not supposed to be a bush," Dr Trifle said, snipping another branch. "See if you can guess what it is."

"Dudley's meant to be catching stray dogs but his eyesight's terrible," Mrs Trifle said. "Last week he brought in three cats, two possums and a rabbit."

"That's it!" Dr Trifle cried. "It's a rabbit! It does look quite like a rabbit, doesn't it?"

"I'm sorry, dear, but it looks more like a

pig eating an ice-cream cone," Mrs Trifle said. "Why are you doing all this?"

"It's called *topiary*," Dr Trifle said to Mrs Trifle. "It's the art of making bushes and shrubs look like something else. I was getting bored with bushes that looked like bushes and shrubs that looked like shrubs."

"Why can't people just let things look like what they are?" Selby thought as he moved out of the sun and under his favourite bush only to have Dr Trifle lop off the shadiest branch.

"Just out of curiosity," Mrs Trifle said, suddenly forgetting about the near-sighted part-time dog catcher and noticing the bush behind her, "is that a hippo doing a handstand?"

"Ummm, er," Dr Trifle said, reaching around and cutting off a big limb. "It's supposed to be a kangaroo juggling three koalas."

"And that one? It looks like a giraffe climbing a ladder."

"Two snakes kissing," Dr Trifle corrected her.

"Surely that one's a cow tying her shoelaces."

"Wrong again. It's the prime minister giving a speech," Dr Trifle said with a sigh. "I'm not very good at this, am I?"

"I'll invite him over tonight and give him a good talking to," Mrs Trifle said.

"Who? The prime minister?"

"Goodness no. Dudley Dewmop. He refuses to wear his new glasses because he says they make his nose itch. I'll just have to insist that he does. As it is, he can't tell a dog from a rabbit."

That night when the near-sighted part-time dog catcher was about to arrive, Selby crept out to the backyard to avoid him.

"Dudley Dewmop, sheeesh!" Selby groaned as he looked around in the moonlight at the eerie animal shapes in the garden, and remembered all the times he'd been chased by the dog catcher. "The man hates dogs!"

Selby lay down under a bush that looked very like a lizard doing a somersault when Dudley Dewmop came driving down the driveway. Which would have been okay if the near-sighted Dudley hadn't missed the driveway entirely and shot straight past the house and into the backyard.

"Gads!" Dudley exclaimed in a loud whisper as he grabbed his dog-catching net and leaped from the car. "I'm surrounded by stray dogs!"

Dudley swung hard at the nearest bush, breaking off four branches at a single hit.

"Gotcha!" he said, plucking sticks and leaves out of his net. "Ooops! Where'd you go?"

SELBY SCREAMS

Selby watched as Dudley raised his net again and again, smashing away at Dr Trifle's topiary. "I see you," the short-sighted dog catcher said, not seeing Selby at all but whacking off the trunk of an elephant and two humps off a camel. "You can't fool me."

Selby watched as Dudley's swishing net

left a litter of leaves on the lawn.

"If I don't stop him," Selby muttered, scooting under another bush only to have it demolished by Dudley, "there won't be a patch of shade left in the whole yard! Help! What can I do?"

Just then a cloud covered the moon and cast the yard into total darkness. Selby stepped towards Dudley and put his paws on his hips knowing that the dog catcher couldn't possibly see him.

"Okay, Dudley," Selby said aloud, "stop it this instant! Enough is enough. You're destroying the Trifle's backyard and they're not going to be very pleased. These aren't stray dogs, they're bushes, you nit!"

"Who said that?" Dudley said, raising his net over his head.

"I did," Selby said calmly and then, just as Selby was about to leap over the fence and escape, the moon came out again and, when it did, Dudley's net came crashing down around him.

"You talked! An animal talked!" Dudley screamed. "And I caught you! People are going to have to pay squillions just to see you! I'm going to be famous!"

"What *is* going on here?" Dr Trifle yelled as he and Mrs Trifle ran out into the backyard and looked around at all the mess. "Dudley, what have you done?"

"Look! He talked!" Dudley cried, pointing at Selby. "He really did! He's a real, live, talking monkey!"

Dr and Mrs Trifle looked at one another and then at the dog catcher.

"Congratulations, Dudley. You've finally caught a dog," Mrs Trifle said, letting Selby out of the net. "Even if he isn't a stray dog. Now could you do me a big favour and put on your new glasses?"

"Maybe you'd better talk to him about his hearing," Dr Trifle whispered to Mrs Trifle. "He seems to be hearing talking monkeys."

"I'll put them on if you wish, Mrs Mayor," Dudley said, putting on the glasses and looking around for a talking monkey but seeing only topiary. "My goodness! Look at all those bushes! They look just like animals."

"Well at least they did before you came along," Dr Trifle muttered.

"That looks just like a bear on a bicycle," Dudley said.

"Does it really?" Dr Trifle asked, taking a closer look.

"It certainly does. And there's a frog in a spacesuit and two dingoes dancing and an emu on a tightrope. They're wonderful, Dr Trifle."

"Are they really?" Dr Trifle asked with a blush.

"Absolutely. I've never seen anything like them before," Dudley said. "Hmmmmmmm, I wonder where that talking monkey went."

"Talking monkey indeed!" Selby muttered, as he ran off down Bunya-Bunya Crescent. "That's the last time I let that dim-witted dog catcher make a monkey out of me."

BOGUSVILLE'S BOXING BALLET

It was the annual Bogusville Charity Night and once again the two bush boxers, Nigel "Knuckles" and Sigmund "Slugfest" were in the dressing-room getting ready for the big fight.

"I'm pleased that you've come once again to help us raise money for our needy," Mrs Trifle said to the huge men and their tiny manager, Wilma "Willy" Wynn. "Many people have paid to see this boxing match tonight and of course the profits will go to charity. Though I have to admit I don't care for fighting myself."

"Mrs Mayor!" Wilma exclaimed, letting her cigar fall from her lips. "Bite your tongue! Boxing is a wonderful sport. It's good exercise and it gives boxers a lot of pleasure."

"Mostly the winners, I should think," Mrs Trifle said, looking around the room for

Selby and wondering where he'd gone. "Now I'd better get back to my seat for the big match. Happy boxing."

In a minute, the dressing-room was empty except for Knuckles, Slugfest, Wilma and Selby—who had hidden in a box in the corner for a close-up view of Knuckles, his favourite boxer.

"All right, boys," Wilma said, spitting into a bucket. "I want you to get out there and beat each other to a pulp. The crowd wants to see lots of blood so give it to them and have a great time! May the best man win."

"Oh, Ma, do we have to?" Knuckles whined. "Do we have to hurt each other?"

"Goodness!" Selby thought. "Knuckles called her *Ma*. Willy Wynn, the manager, must be his mother! This is a surprise."

"Of course you do. Don't be silly."

"But why?"

"Because they've already paid us for the fight, that's why."

"Well I don't care," Knuckles answered. "Slugfest is my brother and I don't want to fight him any more."

"Double goodness," Selby said, stretching his neck for a better look. "Knuckles and Slugfest are brothers and Willy's their mother."

"You just don't want to fight because you

know I'll beat you this time, you big sook," Slugfest said in a deep growl. "I'll knock you out right now if you're not careful!"

"Save it for the ring, boys," Wilma said, stepping between her sons. "There aren't any paying customers in here. Now let's get out there."

"Right you are, Mum." Slugfest turned to Knuckles. "I'm going out there and you'd better come too."

With this he stormed out of the dressing-room nearly knocking over Selby's box as he passed.

"I'm tired of fighting, Mum," Knuckles said. "I never wanted to be a boxer. You made me do it. I only ever wanted to be a ballet dancer."

"Ballet dancer. Don't be silly. That's not fun like punching people. Besides, it's bad for you. It gives people square toes."

"No it doesn't, Ma. It's fun. You should have let me do it. I could have been somebody. I could have been a choreographer."

"A corry-what? They kicked you out of ballet class because you were no good. You couldn't stand on your toes, remember?"

"I know, Ma," Knuckles whimpered. "But I don't like beating people up any more —not even my own brother. I want to stop.

I've been hit so much already that my head's going wonky. One more punch and I'll start hearing voices, for sure. Oh, please, please, please," he added, getting down on his knees.

"Poor Knuckles," Selby thought as a tear trickled down Knuckles' face. "My favourite boxer hates to box."

"I'm sorry," Wilma said, giving Knuckles a pat on the back that could have knocked over an elephant. "I don't mind if you retire from the ring but not tonight. Now I'm going out there right now and I'll count to ten. If you're not there, you know what you'll get."

"No, Ma, please!" Knuckles pleaded. "Not a spanking! No! It's not fair! Nobody spanks like you!"

Wilma strode out of the dressing-room.

"This is awful!" Selby thought. "I've got to do something. I've got to give Knuckles a good pep talk."

"Pull yourself together, Champ," Selby said. "I've got an idea."

Knuckles wiped the tears from his eyes with his boxing gloves and looked around.

"Who's there?" he asked. "Oh, no! I was right! Now I'm hearing things. I've had one punch too many."

"Never mind about that," Selby said from deep inside the box. "Tonight you're going to dance."

"I'm going to what?" Knuckles said to an empty locker.

"Dance, you big lug," Selby said. "You're not going to punch, you're going to dance. If you're a good dancer, he won't be able to lay a glove on you."

"What if I'm not a good dancer?" Knuckles said to the sink.

"Just remember what they taught you at ballet school," Selby said. "Now get out there, your mum's already counted up to nine."

"Oh, no!" Knuckles screeched. "Not another spanking!"

Knuckles raced out of the dressing-room and into the ring as Selby sneaked into the hall. The referee rang the bell and the two boxers came towards each other. Slugfest

threw a punch and watched as his brother hopped to one side. He swung again and Knuckles jumped back as fast as lightning.

"Hey! What's going on here?" Slugfest muttered as a brilliant uppercut missed his dancing brother.

The crowd went silent as Knuckles leaped from side to side and then all around his bewildered brother, who punched in every direction.

"Stand still!" Slugfest whispered. "This isn't fair! We're supposed to be punching each other."

"That's what you think," Knuckles whispered back, spinning around and holding his hands together over his head.

Round after round, Knuckles danced as the sweat poured off his brawny brother.

"Make him stand still," Slugfest hissed at the referee.

"There's nothing in the rules about standing still," the referee said as Knuckles picked him up and spun him around, putting him back on the canvas ever so gently.

Slugfest drew in a deep breath and then punched in every direction as fast as he could, hoping to hit his brother just by luck.

"Ha ha, you can't hit me," Knuckles sang as he danced this way and that, and the crowd roared as the exhausted Slugfest collapsed on the canvas.

"What a fight!" the referee yelled, holding up Knuckles' hand. "You've won! I've never seen anything like it! It was a no-punch fight!"

"I did it!" Knuckles screamed at his smiling mother. "Did you see me dance on my toes, Ma! Now they'll have to let me back into ballet class!"

"Ma? Ballet class?" the smiling Mrs Trifle mumbled as she and Selby started home. "Am I hearing things?"

"If you are," Selby thought as he trotted alongside her, "you're not the first one to hear things tonight."

SELBY TIPPED TO WIN

It was a happy day for Bogusville when the international domino tipping-over champion, Sandra "Steady" Sturgis stabbed a finger at the map of the world and said, "Right there is where I will construct the domino tipping-over show of the century and win back the highly coveted diamond-studded World Domino Tipping-Over Trophy from that nasty little country that I'd rather you didn't mention."

"But, Steady," her domino coach said as he brushed the pink velvet on her best domino setting-up trousers, "your finger has just landed on Australia."

"Not just Australia," Steady said, sliding her finger to the side to see the tiny letters underneath, "but a town called Bogusville. It's the perfect place. All I have to do is talk the mayor into letting us use one of the public buildings for the domino show."

"I don't understand," Mrs Trifle said when Steady Sturgis and her coach came to see her about the contest.

"It's simple," said Steady, looking over at Selby who lay on the carpet nearby. "Remember when you were a child and you set up a line of dominoes and then tipped one over and they all went down like ... like dominoes?"

"Yes, but—" Mrs Trifle started.

"Well things have changed," said the coach, who was standing stiffly behind Steady.

"Changed?" Selby thought. "Maybe they're making round dominoes now."

"The dominoes themselves haven't changed but the sport of domino tipping-over is now one of the most competitive, highly developed, difficult, brain-taxing, expensive and fun sports in the whole—"

"Yes, Ms Sturgis, I understand all that," Mrs Trifle interrupted. "What I don't understand is why you want to hold your domino spectacular in Bogusville."

"No tremors," Steady said. "No earthquakes. No volcanoes erupting. No bombs going off. Not even a ripple. The ground in Bogusville just sits there. It doesn't move at all."

"I see," Mrs Trifle said, looking down and noticing that the floor in the lounge room wasn't moving.

"The slightest wobble can ruin months of careful domino setting-up just like that!" Steady said, snapping her gloved fingers. "And I'm not taking any chances. The first-ever domino tipping-over contest was held in Tokyo on the day of their biggest earthquake."

"And I believe it rained dominoes for days," Steady's coach said, adding in a low voice: "Don't forget to tell Mayor Trifle about you-know-what."

"Ah, yes, I was coming to that," Steady said. "Here in Bogusville we can keep this whole thing secret till the last minute and that's extremely important."

"Why do you want to keep it secret?" Mrs Trifle asked.

"The world domino tipping-over title is now held by a nasty little country that I'd rather not mention. They cheated me out of it last year. Their spies sneaked into the exhibition hall and started my dominoes tipping over the night before the judging. There was no time to set them up again for the judges to see."

"You're afraid they might do the same again, is that it?" Mrs Trifle asked.

"You are an incredibly understanding and intelligent woman, Mrs Mayor. Now is it okay if I use your town hall?" Steady asked. "On the day of the tipping-over, we'll invite every man, woman and dog in Bogusville to see the spectacle of a lifetime."

"That would be very nice," Mrs Trifle said, looking over at Selby. "But maybe we'd better forget the dogs. They might start things tipping by accident."

"Quite right," Steady said. "And remember, with all the press coverage, this will truly put Bogusville on the map."

"Of course you can use the town hall," Mrs Trifle said, wondering how Steady and her coach had found their way to Bogusville if it wasn't on the map. "I can't see what harm it'll do."

"Yahooooooooo!" Steady screamed, kissing Mrs Trifle on both cheeks. "You'll never regret this. Come on, Coach, we'd better get moving."

The next day a truckload of dominoes in every size and colour arrived and Steady began setting them up.

"That Steady is quite a woman," Dr Trifle said to Mrs Trifle one evening when there wasn't much else to say. "I've never known anyone to work so hard. But I'm a bit concerned about the town hall. Did you know that she's locked it all up and no one's allowed in?"

"Yes, I know," Mrs Trifle said, as she put some Dry-Mouth Dog Biscuits in Selby's bowl. "And when the council and I go into the council chambers we all have to tiptoe so we don't start the dominoes tipping. But Steady will have to be finished setting them up by ten o'clock tomorrow morning. The World Domino Tipping-Over jury came to town today and they're ready for the judging. If she's not ready tomorrow, they'll all fly back to where they came from and the trophy will stay in that country that Steady would rather not mention."

"I only hope that the people of Bogusville enjoy the show," Dr Trifle said.

"I'm sure they will," Mrs Trifle said, patting Selby's head. "In fact, Steady has invited us both over to the hall tonight for a look at the dominoes. Come along."

"I'm sure the *people* of Bogusville will enjoy the show," Selby thought as he sneaked over to the town hall after the Trifles had left the house. "But I thought Mrs Trifle's remark about dogs starting the dominoes tipping was quite unfair."

The lights in the hall were on when Selby climbed a nearby tree and peered through a window. The floor was black with lines of dominoes and Dr and Mrs Trifle stood quietly at a safe distance. He watched as Steady Sturgis took the last domino from a velvet cushion held by her coach and put it down.

"Finished!" she yelled. "Seventy-two million dominoes set to go! When the jury arrives in the morning, I will lie on the floor, resting on an elbow, and with the flick of a finger I'll knock over the starter domino and it'll be on for young and old. First there will be one row falling and then two and then three! Then on to the Rainbow Run!"

"The Rainbow Run?" Mrs Trifle said.

"When those dominoes over there begin to fall there'll be a cascade of colour like a hundred rainbows sweeping up and over the archway. You will need sunglasses just to look at them. Then down to the Sea of Sorrows."

"The Sea of Sorrows?" Dr Trifle said.

"Huge waves of dominoes will flow back and forth across the main floor, crashing on rocks made of dominoes and setting up a wind that will blow the jury's hats off! Then on to the Circle of Fire!"

"The Circle of Fire?" Mrs Trifle said.

"Round and round they'll go in that big bowl, all rubbing together as they fall, throwing up sparks until they ignite in a mass of flames! And then, finally, on to the Musical Map!"

"The Musical Map?" Dr Trifle said.

"See that big slope over there? A line of dominoes will snake around to the top of the rectangle and then the whole mass of them will begin to topple. The sides of all the dominoes are painted so that as they fall you'll see the map of Australia suddenly appear. But that's not all! Each domino is specially made to play a musical note when it falls, so as the map appears you will hear 'Advance Australia Fair' so loud that you'll have to put your fingers in your ears!"

"Wow!" Selby said as Steady and the Trifles locked up and tiptoed out of the hall. "The Rainbow Run, the Sea of Sorrows, the Circle of Fire and the Musical Map! I'll stay right here till morning and watch it through the window. If I can only (yawn) stay awake."

No sooner were the words out of Selby's mouth than he slumped over the branch and fell sound asleep, only to be wakened by whispers from the hall.

"Grimblerk, look!" a voice said. "The dominoes is all set up to fall down! He he he he (snort) heh heh! We knock'em all over now."

"Too right, little Ogglebriff," another voice said. "We knock'em all down like accident and we keep'em highly coveted diamond-studded trophy. Heh heh heh (snort)."

119

"Grimblerk? Ogglebriff?" Selby thought as he peered in at the two men who had broken into the town hall. "They must be spies from that country that Steady would rather not mention. I've got to stop them before they start the dominoes tipping!"

With this, Selby let out a great scream and swung from his branch, crashing through the window, causing the two spies—who had never seen a screaming, swinging dog before—to faint. All of which would have been okay if he hadn't landed smack on the starter domino and started the line of dominoes toppling.

"Oh, no!" Selby yelled as he ran along the line of tipping dominoes, trying to head them off only to have them branch out into two lines and then three. "If I don't stop them, Steady won't win back the trophy!"

Selby tore ahead, diving into the middle of the Rainbow Run only to have the tipping dominoes spread around him in a blinding cascade of colour.

"Stop!" Selby screamed, wishing he was wearing sunglasses. "No, not the Sea of Sorrows!" he added, picking himself up too late and diving onto the floor of the Sea of Sorrows with waves of dominoes crashing left and right.

"I'll have to head it off at the Circle of

Fire!" Selby screeched as he jumped into the bowl just as the first dominoes started to fall against one another, throwing up more and

more sparks until tiny flames came and went all around him.

For a moment there was silence. Selby stood up and looked around.

"I did it!" he thought. "I stopped the dominoes tipping over. Of course it's a catastrophe—but at least it's only a little catastrophe and not a big one."

Selby sniffed the air.

"Ooooooops! There's something still burning," he thought. "I wonder what it could be? Yikes! My foot's on fire!" he yelled, jumping out of the Ring of Fire and stamping the ground. "Oh no! I've started the dominoes tipping again! They're headed for the top of the Musical Map. It's my last chance to rescue any of the domino tipping-over spectacular!"

Selby raced after the line of falling dominoes and then threw himself through the air, snatching at the top domino of the map but overshooting and crashing straight out the back door. He picked himself up and turned around just in time to hear the last deafening bars of "Advance Australia Fair" and see Steady Sturgis, her coach and the jury dash into the hall in their dressing-gowns.

"I'm ruined!" Steady screamed as she threw herself on the domino-littered floor. "I'd go mad if I had to set them all up again! This is the end of my career!"

"Just a minute," the president of the jury said, looking at the unconscious men. "I'd know these two rascals anywhere. This is Grimblerk and Ogglebriff from that nasty little country that now holds the trophy. It must have been they who started the dominoes toppling. And because they cheated, I hearby award the highly coveted diamond-studded World Domino Tipping-Over Trophy to you."

"Thank you so much," Steady said, snatching the trophy. "I'm only sorry that every man, woman and dog in Bogusville missed the show."

"Every man and woman in Bogusville may have missed the show," Selby thought as he sped off home. "But this little doggie didn't miss a thing."

SELBY FLIES
THE SMILING SKIES

"You're a naughty dog getting my boys all excited like that!" Aunt Jetty said as she watched her sons, Willy and Billy, chase Selby round and round the lounge room with their wooden tomahawks. "I'm putting you on the first plane to where the Trifles are staying, even if they are on holidays."

"Mummy, he talks," Willy wailed as he shot a rubber-tipped arrow at Selby. "I heard him talk once and I'm going to make him talk again."

"Yes, yes, dear," Aunt Jetty said. "I'm sure you did. Now stop that playing, I'm taking Selby to the airport."

"Thank goodness!" Selby thought as Willy's lasso missed him by a millimetre. "I can't wait to get away from these horrible people and back with the Trifles. And I'll get to fly in an aeroplane for the first time! Oh boy!"

"I only wish I could send Willy and Billy along too," Aunt Jetty mumbled. "Then it would be really peaceful around here."

On the way to the airport, Selby remembered the ads he'd seen for Happytime Airlines with a beautiful, smiling stewardess fluffing up a passenger's pillow and saying, "We know how to make people happy. Come smile awhile in the happy skies of Happytime."

"She looked *so* friendly and *so* neat," Selby thought. "I hope I'm flying on Happytime. I can't wait to sit back in my seat and have her fluff up my pillow while I eat those cute little meals, watch movies on tiny screens, and look down at people on the ground who are so small they look like ants. It's going to be great!"

Aunt Jetty's truck screeched to a stop and she jumped out and handed Selby over to a Happytime Airlines employee.

"Of course he'll travel in the baggage compartment," the man said, dropping Selby in a wire cage. "But I'm sure he'll be happy in there."

"More's the pity," Aunt Jetty mumbled.

In a minute, Selby found himself travelling along darkened corridors on a conveyor belt surrounded by suitcases.

"It's not fair!" he moaned. "I want to sit in a proper seat. I want to look out the window and see people who look like ants. I want to be a passenger, not a prisoner! Oh, woe, what is a dog to do?"

Selby's mind raced like a runaway train. Suddenly he reached through the cage and undid the latch.

"I know what a dog can do," he thought, jumping out of the cage. "He can get on that plane as a normal passenger, that's what. All I have to do is get a disguise."

Selby pictured himself in a raincoat, wearing a beard and sunglasses and then in a long gown with strings of pearls and a wig.

"Oh, it's no use. No matter what I wear, I'll look like a dog. But hold the show! What's wrong with looking like a dog? I'll dress up as a dog. I'll get a dog costume and people will think I'm a person in a dog suit!" he thought, suddenly remembering the money hidden in his collar that he got for acting in the Dry-Mouth Dog Biscuits ad. "It's perfect! They'll never think it's a dog in a dog suit."

Selby crept into a deserted office, grabbed the telephone book and found an ad that said:

COURAGEOUS COSTUME HIRE

COME HERE FOR YOUR GEAR.

HIRE THE ATTIRE THAT YOU DARE TO WEAR.

126

Selby picked up a telephone and dialled.

"Hello, Courageous Costume? I'm in a bit of a fix and I need a dog costume fast. Bring it to the airport. If you can get it here in ten minutes, you've got a deal."

It was a puzzled delivery man who came into the airport carrying the dog suit and looking around for the mysterious caller. It was a startled delivery man who caught a glimpse of something small and furry as it snatched the parcel and then disappeared into the crowd.

"Hey, what was that? I've been mugged by a midget! Stop, thief!" he yelled, suddenly noticing the money that lay at his feet and picking it up. "Ha ha! The joke's on him! He just dropped enough money to *pay* for the wretched costume. He can keep it."

Selby slipped into the costume, stood on his hind legs and then hurried to the smiling clerk at the Happytime Airlines counter.

"And where are we off to today in our little doggie suit?" the clerk asked, grinning down at Selby.

"I don't know about you but I'm off to Paradise Cove," Selby said. "Make it a half fare, I'm under twelve years old."

"Anything you say," the clerk said, taking the money that Selby had placed on the counter and then smoothing his hair with his fingers. "We know how to make people happy

127

on Happytime Airlines. And you're in luck today, our in-flight snackette is South Seas Caress. Ummmmmmmmmm."

"What is South Seas Caress?"

"Why, coconut custard, of course," the man said, handing Selby his ticket. "Now have a Hap-Hap-Happytime."

"We'll see about that," Selby mumbled as he raced for the plane.

"What a cute little outfit," the friendly stewardess said, showing him to his seat. "Let me fluff up a pillow for you."

"Oh, look! It's true," Selby said, looking out the window. "The people *do* look like ants."

"I'm afraid those *are* ants," the stewardess said, putting the pillow behind Selby's head. "We haven't taken off yet. Now sit back and relax. If you need anything, just push the call-button."

"Oh boy! Oh boy!" Selby thought. "This is the life, flying the happy skies of Happytime Airlines and being looked after by happy people."

Just then the plane tore down the runway and turned up sharply into the sky and in a few minutes a stewardess came down the aisle pulling a squirming boy.

"Why can't I fly the plane?" Willy

screamed. "Why can't I have a go?"

"Oh, no! Aunt Jetty's sending the brat to Paradise Cove to stay with the Trifles!" Selby thought. "The nerve of her!"

"We showed you the cockpit," the stewardess said, looking in a hand mirror and putting on another layer of lipstick, "and now I'll give you a Happytime Airlines colouring-in book."

"I don't want a stupid colouring-in book!" Willy said, suddenly stopping and staring at Selby. "Hey, mister short man, why are you wearing a dog suit?"

"Is it against the law?" Selby asked in a low voice.

"Yes it is!" Willy wailed. "Yes it is against the law!"

"Ease off, kid," Selby said, pretending to read the safety instruction card.

"Take your head off," Willy whined. "I want to see you."

The smiling stewardess brushed her hair until it was in one perfect piece and then gave it a quick spray.

"I'll leave you boys to play," she said, starting away. "I have to prepare the South Seas Caress."

"Take it off, mister stupid!" Willy squealed, grabbing the head of the costume.

"Take your head off!"

"Hey! Let go!" Selby yelled, struggling against Willy's iron grip. "You'll rip it!"

"But I want to see your face!"

"Back off or I'll push the call-button and you'll be dragged back to your seat," Selby said, pushing the call-button to get someone to drag Willy back to his seat.

Suddenly a steward appeared, straightening his necktie and polishing a button on his sleeve.

"Is there something you wish?" he asked, smiling down at Willy who was now on top of Selby and tugging at his costume.

"Yes!" Selby screeched. "Tie this little monster up and gag him! If you want me to smile awhile, that'll do it."

The steward stopped smiling for a minute and then burst out laughing.

"Oh, ho ho ho ho ho. For a minute I thought you were serious," he said as he blew a microscopic piece of lint off his shoulder. "Keep right on having a Hap-Hap-Happytime, boys. See you later."

"Won't anyone take a guy in a dog suit seriously," Selby thought as Willy lifted the head of his costume for an instant.

"So it's you!" Willy yelled. "You talked! I knew you could talk! Hey, everybody," Willy yelled to the passengers, "look at the talking dog!"

Everyone put their newspapers down for a second and then pulled them back up again. Then, in the instant that Willy's back was turned, Selby got up and started slowly down the aisle.

"Hey! Don't you try to get away from

me!" Willy screamed, running after him. Willy twirled his lasso in the air and Selby broke into an awkward run just ahead of him.

"I'm done," Selby thought. "I can't handle him myself. Somehow I've got to get the cabin crew to keep him away from me."

"When I catch you," Willy squealed, "I'm going to take your head off and everyone will know you're a talking dog! You just wait!"

A grinning steward and a stewardess stepped out of the way, straightening their suits and watching as Willy chased Selby round and round the inside of the plane.

"Why do all these Happytime Airlines people have to be so happy all the time," Selby thought, squeezing around a food trolley. "If they were normal grumpy people they wouldn't put up with Willy for a second. I wonder if there's a Grumpytime Airlines ...?"

"Yaaaahhhhooooo!" Willy screamed and he jumped over the trolley, making the steward and stewardess laugh with delight.

Selby rounded a corner and dived under a seat.

"I can't believe all this silly smiling stuff," he thought as he crawled from one seat to the next. "It's got to be an act."

"Come here, talking doggie!" Willy yelled. "Wild West Willy will find you!"

"It's just not normal for people to be this happy all the time," Selby thought, suddenly reaching out and tripping Willy. "They've got to have their limits."

Selby watched as Willy went flying down the aisle and crashed headfirst into a food trolley, throwing little plastic bowls of South Seas Caress in every direction.

"That's funny!" Willy laughed. "Look at the funny gooey people. Ha ha ha ha ha ha."

There was a deathly silence as an angry stewardess picked a handful of coconut custard out of her hair.

"You monster!" she screamed. "You've ruined my hair!"

"And my uniform!" the steward cried, scraping custard off the front of his suit. "Now it'll have to be dry-cleaned!"

"That does it!" said the stewardess as she grabbed Willy by the hair. "Goodbye smile-awhile! Put a gag in the brat's mouth while I tie him up with his rope."

"I didn't do anything! No, don't put that gag in my mmmmooooonnggggguuu!" the struggling Willy cried.

Selby slipped back into his seat and watched as they carried Willy to his seat and strapped him in. A cheer and a round of applause went up all around the plane.

"Well I'll say one thing for Happytime Airlines," Selby said as he fluffed his own pillow and put on some headphones to listen to the movie, "they certainly know how to make people happy—all of them but Willy, that is."

SELBY IN LOVE

It was a sunny spring day and Selby lay in the shade of his favourite bush, finishing a book he'd found called *Love Dawns Eternal*. A warm wind sprang up just as he read the last paragraph.

For a year I'd worked for Howard Cooper, the master of Cooper's Rest. He was a man both silent and strong. Howard, whose dark looks cried out for a woman's love, my love. And now, as I was about to board the coach and leave forever, I turned back a loose strand of hair and Howard caught a glimpse of my rose-coloured fingernails. Then his eyes penetrated my soul and he gently clasped my hands. His quiet voice whispered in my ear, "Oh Dawn, my rosy-fingered Dawn, you are the one I've waited for these many years. Please don't go. Stay on and be my wife."

"Oh, that sends shivers up my spine," Selby

said with a sigh. "Imagine. For all that time Howard didn't even notice her and then his eyes penetrated her soul (sigh) and he fell instantly in love (sigh). Oh, isn't love wonderful," Selby thought as he tripped lightly into the house and lay dreamily on the carpet. "I only wish it could happen to me. Why can't I find someone like Dawn to fall in love with?"

And then it was that Selby heard out of the corner of his ear, Mrs Trifle say to Dr Trifle, "Did you know that your old friend, Ralpho, is having a rather successful tour of country towns?"

"Ralpho? *The* Ralpho?" Dr Trifle asked, referring to his old friend Ralpho the Magnificent, failed inventor and sometimes magician. "I thought after the disastrous show he put on here for the boy scouts and girl guides, he would have gone out of the magic business for good."

"For everyone's good," thought Selby, who remembered rescuing Ralpho from his robot-mummy.

"He not only didn't quit," Mrs Trifle said, "he seems to have added a talking dog to his act."

"A talking dog?" Selby wondered. "How can it be? I'm the only talking dog in Australia and perhaps the world."

"A talking dog?" Dr Trifle asked. "How could it be? There aren't any talking dogs in the whole world—not even in Australia."

"I know that, dear," Mrs Trifle said. "He rang to invite us to his show and he said that his dog was a *real* version of your talking robot-dog."

"My what?"

"The poor man was so flustered when he was here last that he went away with the impression that Selby was some sort of robot."

"Now I remember," Dr Trifle said, trying to snap his fingers the way people do sometimes when they remember something. "He *said* he was going to build a robot-dog like that horrible mummy thing. He's undoubtedly got a stuffed-toy dog with a tape recorder in it. My guess is that it'll look like a toy and it'll sound like a tape recorder and it won't fool anyone. But I have to admit, that mummy wasn't bad before it went out of control."

"There's an article about Ralpho here in the newspaper," Mrs Trifle said, holding up a copy of the *Bogusville Banner*. "In it he says Lulu was found—"

"Lulu?"

"His talking dog. The article says that Lulu is a real live talking dog who was found walking aimlessly in the jungles of the Amazon."

"That's the sort of thing Ralpho might say to get people to go along and see his act, don't you think?"

"Well, maybe," Mrs Trifle said. "But if that's true, he's managed to fool everyone in the towns he's been to on his tour and Melanie Mildew as well."

"Melanie Mildew?" Dr Trifle asked.

"She's the one who wrote the article," Mrs Trifle said, "and I don't think she's easy to fool."

"Gulp," Selby thought, "neither do I. I wonder if there could be any truth in this."

"I just wonder if there could be any truth in this," Dr Trifle said. "I guess we'll have to trot along tonight and see for ourselves."

"Yes," Mrs Trifle said, "and Ralpho asked us to bring Selby along. Why not, he might enjoy it."

That night the Trifles and Selby sat in the front row of the Bogusville Bijou as Ralpho's show went terribly wrong. First one of his juggling rings got caught on a light and wouldn't come down. Then he tried to juggle three bowling pins but one hit him on the head and the other two landed on his toes. And when he talked to his ventriloquist's dummy his mouth was moving so much that the audience screamed with laughter, making it impossible for anyone to hear anything.

"Quiet please!" Ralpho yelled as he put the dummy away and got out a whip. "Now if I may have a volunteer from the audience I will demonstrate how I can take a pencil out of someone's mouth at ten metres with the crack of this whip. Come on, speak up. Who will it be?"

For a minute, no one moved and then a voice cried out, "Well it won't be me! Fair crack of the whip, Ralpho, you'd take my head off and leave the pencil!"

"Poor Ralpho," Selby thought as the audience burst into laughter, "he's just not a showman."

"Okay," Ralpho said, pulling out a pistol, "I guess that brings us to the trick-shooting part of my act."

Suddenly there was a stampede for the exits which only stopped when Mrs Trifle leaped to the stage and grabbed the microphone.

"Come back, everyone! Please! Order! Order," she yelled. "Ralpho's not going to do his trick-shooting act, are you Ralpho?"

"I don't know why no one likes my trick shooting," Ralpho muttered to Mrs Trifle.

"It's always so exciting. I think so anyway. Okay, I'll bring out the talking dog and finish the act."

"Ladies and gentlemen," Mrs Trifle said, stepping aside, "can we have a big hand for Lulu the talking dog!"

Ralpho reached down and lifted a small dog onto the table in front of him.

"Hmmmmmmm," Selby thought, pricking up his ears. "That doesn't look like a stuffed toy. It looks like the real thing. But of course it can't be. It'll be interesting to see how Ralpho fakes the talking part."

Ralpho pulled a watch out of his pocket.

"Excuse me, folks," he said, looking at his watch, "but I've got a train to catch in just a few minutes and I don't want to miss it.

"Now let me tell you about Lulu. She was found wandering aimlessly in the jungles of the Amazon by a butterfly collector from Ballarat who later sold her to me," Ralpho said. "He was on his way out of the jungle after collecting seventy-two new species of butterfly when he happened across her. He reached down to pat her and she said in perfect English, 'Excuse me, sir, but I'm lost.' Didn't you, Lulu?"

"That's correct," the dog said suddenly in perfect English.

"It's got to be a trick. She's hardly moving her mouth," Selby thought, suddenly remembering that he hardly moved his mouth when he talked. "She can't be a real talking dog. There simply aren't any—well, except for yours truly."

"Tell the audience more about yourself," Ralpho said.

"There isn't really anything to tell, Mr Magnificent," Lulu said. "I have amnesia and can't remember anything before I met the butterfly collector."

"So there you have it, folks," Ralpho said. "The only talking dog in the world!"

"My goodness," Dr Trifle whispered to Mrs Trifle loud enough for Selby to hear as well. "This is the most sophisticated piece of gadgetry I've had the pleasure of seeing. I wonder how he's doing it? I think we can rule out the use of a super high-frequency oscillating converter."

"Can we?" Mrs Trifle asked.

"Yes. And we can also rule out lambda wave transmission through thixotropic media."

"Are you sure?"

"Absolutely. And he couldn't be using smart-quark excitation because I don't suppose he's ever even heard of it," Dr Trifle said.

"Do you know those silly dolls that have a string you pull to make them talk?" Mrs Trifle asked. "I think it's one of those."

"Hmmm, good point," Dr Trifle said, looking for a string but not seeing any.

"I know what you're all thinking," Ralpho said, glancing at his watch again. "You think that Lulu has a string I pull to make her talk. Not true, is it Lulu?"

"No, it certainly isn't, Mr Magnificent," Lulu giggled.

"And now, ladies and gentlemen," Ralpho said, "I need a different sort of volunteer. Could you please bring your dog up here, Dr and Mrs Trifle?"

Mrs Trifle picked up Selby and put him on the table next to Lulu.

"Hello, how are you?" Lulu said, and Selby felt himself go all weak at the knees.

"I can't believe it," Selby thought as he looked deep into Lulu's eyes. "It sounded like she actually spoke to me!"

Ralpho looked at his watch for a moment and then said, "What do you think of the mayor's dog, Lulu?"

"He's very handsome," Lulu said, batting her eyelids.

"I can't believe it!" Selby thought. "Here I am face to face with another talking dog! A friend at last! Maybe even a girlfriend!"

"I think he thinks you're very pretty," Ralpho said.

"Do you think so, Mr Magnificent?"
"Oh, wonder of wonders!" Selby thought.
"This is the most beautiful day of my life."

"Go ahead, little doggie," Ralpho said to Selby. "Don't be shy. Talk to her. She won't bite. Ha ha ha."

The audience giggled and then burst into spontaneous applause.

"Lulu is a thinking, feeling and talking dog just like me!" Selby thought. "I've got to talk to her before Ralpho races off to catch that train. But—but—but if I do my secret will be out. Who knows—I could end up in Ralpho's show!"

"I like you," Lulu said, blinking her eyelashes at Selby. "Do you like me?"

Selby saw a tiny smile cross Lulu's lips and his mind raced like a speeding train.

"Oh, no! Her eyes just penetrated my soul!" he thought. "If I don't talk to her now I'll miss my chance. She'll never know that there's another talking dog in the world!"

Selby was just about to say: "My name's Selby and I believe that you and I are the only talking dogs in Australia and perhaps the world," when suddenly Lulu said, "Thank you for sharing your thoughts with me, with me, with me, with me, with me—"

There was a murmur in the crowd as Ralpho kicked something under the table and then there was a terrible scratching noise.

"It's not a talking dog at all!" someone screamed. "Ralpho's got a record-player under the table! Look!"

"I see!" Dr Trifle said to Mrs Trifle. "He knows exactly when she's going to speak and he asks her questions just before she answers. It's the oldest trick in the book."

"Thank you, ladies and gentlemen," Ralpho said, turning bright red and running off with Lulu as the audience roared with laughter.

"It's a pity about that record-player getting stuck," Mrs Trifle said later when they were walking home. "Poor old Ralpho almost had me believing that there was a real talking dog right here in Bogusville."

"Yes," Dr Trifle said. "He certainly gave us all something to think about for a minute or so."

"One more minute," Selby thought as he trotted ahead, "and I'd have given them something to really think about!"

Whoa!

Hold on a minute. Don't put the book down yet. Sometimes when I'm on the phone to the author he tells me about your letters. Lots of you think I'm your dog. No, Jenny, my name's not really Sparky and I don't live with you. Sorry. So stop trying to make Sparky confess. You'll drive him crazy. The best way to drive a thinking, feeling dog bonkers is to yap at him all the time. If he was really me you'd see certain signs.

Turn the page for some hints on recognizing talking dogs.

See ya!

Selby

SEVEN WARNING SIGNS
OF A TALKING DOG

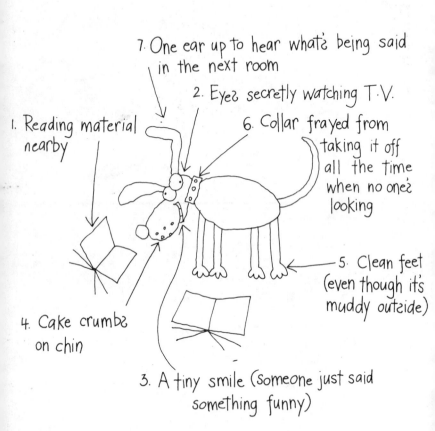

7. One ear up to hear what's being said in the next room

2. Eyes secretly watching T.V.

1. Reading material nearby

6. Collar frayed from taking it off all the time when no one's looking

5. Clean feet (even though it's muddy outside)

4. Cake crumbs on chin

3. A tiny smile (someone just said something funny)